HIS PAIN

WRATH JAMES WHITE

deadite
press

DEADITE PRESS
205 NE BRYANT
PORTLAND, OR 97211
www.DEADITEPRESS.com

AN ERASERHEAD PRESS COMPANY
www.ERASERHEADPRESS.com

ISBN: 1-936383-67-5

Printed in the USA.

*"Nothing begins and nothing ends
that is not paid in moan;
For we are born in other's pain,
and perish in our own."*

—Francis Thompson, *"Daisy"*

Something ripped as Melanie contracted both her abdominal and kegel muscles and pushed with all she was worth. The infant split open her sex as its body progressed through her cervix, dilating it as if she were being raped by an elephant. Seven pounds, eight ounces, nineteen inches, tore slowly through an opening that had previously admitted nothing larger than eight inches.

"Aaaaaeeeiiii! Oh God! I can't take it! Aaaaaarrgh!"

"The head is crowning! I can see it. Keep pushing!"

The doctor held up a mirror so she could see her vagina tear wide and disgorge the mewling parasite she'd carried within her for nine months. Her eyes rolled up in her head and she let out another terse scream as she squeezed out the child's head and shoulders.

"AAAAAaaaaah! AAAAAaaaaah!"

"That's it! That's it! It's coming!"

A few more agonizing contractions and Jason slid out into the doctor's arms followed immediately by the chunky red afterbirth.

"It's a boy!" the doctor announced gleefully. He tied off the umbilical chord and snipped it and the baby shrieked like a scalded cat.

His entire body twisted and convulsed as the shrill cry tore from Jason's tiny lungs. The piercing scream emptying the small child of all vitality. He shook spasmodically, frothing at the mouth, his eyes rolling up into his head. Then he lay still, dangling lifelessly in the doctor's arms.

"Is that normal? Is he okay? What's wrong with our baby?" Edward asked frantically.

The doctor stood holding the little boy's limp body, looking from nurse to nurse in shock, like a child who'd accidentally broken something valuable and knew he'd be blamed for it.

"He's not breathing. Bring the crash cart over STAT!"

"What's wrong? What's wrong with my baby?"

Melanie was panicking now too. She sat up in bed with her legs still in the stirrups and her face imploring the doctor for answers. She was spent and fatigued, but she could not let herself sleep until she knew her child was okay.

Melanie reached out for her husband and they hugged each other for comfort, watching as their newborn baby disappeared into a throng of nurses and doctors urgently working to save the child's life.

Their baby was whisked away to an emergency room and Melanie was led into a nearby recovery room with Edward still at her side trying to comfort her.

"These doctors are professionals. I'm sure they deal with this kind of thing every day. I know our baby will be fine. God looks out for the little ones."

But Melanie could see his own worry and stress behind his optimistic façade. When he began to pray, rather than console her as it was meant to, it only increased her concern.

Four hours went by before the doctor returned with news of their son's health.

"We're not sure what's wrong with him. All of his vitals seem normal. His heart, lungs, liver, and kidney are well-developed and strong. We did a CAT scan that confirmed normal brain function although there was some elevated activity in the Thalamus that we have a Neurologist looking at now. His blood-pressure is also rather elevated and he's pumping adrenaline like a prizefighter. He—he appears to be in pain, a lot of pain. We just can't identify the source."

The first year of Jason's life was spent screaming in mind-numbing anguish as his parents held him, rocked him, and sang to him. Their soft cooing voices lanced through his eardrums and rattled in his skull. The press of their flesh against his, the heat of their bodies, the swaying motion as they walked with him in their arms felt like he was in a car wreck being tossed around as the vehicle tumbled down an embankment and burned.

"He screams every time I touch him, every time I speak

to him. From the time he wakes up to the time he goes to sleep he just screams and cries! He even cries when I try to feed him. He doesn't love me. He- he hates me!" His mother cried to one specialist after another as they examined her tortured child with looks of utter perplexity on their faces.

Everything hurt. The feel of the blankets abrading his delicate skin, the scalding heat of daylight searing through the chips in the black paint that coated the windows, the smell of human sweat, breath, excrement, deodorant, and hair products, the jangling cacophony of the human voice, his own included. The feel of polluted oxygen raking its way down his throat into his lungs felt to him like breathing teargas. The expanding of his lungs felt as if his chest were being torn open. Every sound, every taste, every scent, every sensation his body absorbed hit him like an assault. At times the beating of his own heart made him want to scream.

It took several examinations and innumerable tedious and excruciating tests before all the specialists reached a probable diagnosis.

"Your child has Acute Hypersensitivity. It's a rare form of a very rare disorder, a type of Thalamic Syndrome or Central Pain Disorder. Usually it's caused by damage to the Thalamus, the part of your brain where sensory information is processed, but your son seems to have been born with it. To put it simply, his nervous system is wired up improperly sending an overload of signals to the pain centers of his brain. Every sensation he feels registers in his brain as physical distress. It's highly unlikely that he'll live more than a few years and he'll probably spend all of that time in agony. We can give him pain-killers and keep increasing the dosages and switching medications as he builds up tolerances, but eventually we will run out of drugs powerful enough to help. By that time he'll also be hopelessly addicted."

"You mean he's going to be addicted to narcotics for the rest of his life?"

"Either that or in constant agony."

His parents did what they could. They had his room insulated against sound intrusion. They had the windows painted black to keep out the sun. They removed the light bulbs from the light fixture in the ceiling and padded the walls and floor with foam rubber.

His food had to be washed and boiled several times to render it tasteless enough for him to consume, then cooled to room temperature. The meat and vegetables were then sliced into pieces so small that he could swallow them without chewing. Everything he ate was chopped, minced, or pureed. The only liquid he could consume was purified water. Still, the act of eating was anathema to him. The entire digestive process was torturous and bowel movements of any kind felt to him as if he were being wrenched inside out.

The drugs helped some. By the age of seventeen he'd been on every narcotic from Codeine to Morphine. His father had even brought him Heroine once or twice when the screaming had become intolerable. Eventually the screaming stopped as Jason acquired a tolerance for the little pain they couldn't protect him from.

"It's cruel to keep him alive. Do you think we're being selfish? Maybe we should just let him die?"

"We can't! Are you crazy? He's our child! Our little boy. We have to help him."

"That's what I'm trying to do. That's all I ever try to do. But maybe we're doing the wrong thing by him. Maybe the best thing we could do would be to end his suffering forever."

Jason sat in his darkened room listening to his parents argue. He had heard this conversation many times over the years, when his parents thought he wasn't listening. Sometimes they would forget to close his bedroom door. His father's heartfelt pleas for his euthanasia made him love the old man. It was an emotion that fit uncomfortably in his heart. His mother's insistence that he continue to live in agony made him hate the bitch.

"Here you go, honey."

Jason winced. His eardrums felt like they'd been punctured with a sewing needle. His mother stood in the doorway to his bedroom holding a rubber cup filled

8

with water. Rubber was the only substance that was not unbearable to him. Other textures felt like sandpaper across raw nerves. In her other hand she held his painkillers. Jason hated taking them. The dry chalky pills felt like battery acid as they burned their way down to his belly, but two or three Darvocets every couple of hours were the only things that kept him from chewing the veins out of his wrists. When the medication inevitably wore out it felt as if he were floating in a pool of fire ants.

"I wish you would put some clothes on. I know they hurt you, but you're too old now to be sitting around the house naked all the time."

Jason ignored her. He knew his stoic silence bothered her, but he was sick of the headaches the jarring vibration of his voice inevitably caused him. Even the Darvocet wasn't enough to help him once the migraines came on. Only sensory deprivation would help then.

His parents had a sensory deprivation device built for him to help quite the noise of the world. It was a latex vacuum body-bag that hung from the ceiling on nylon ropes affixed to each corner. A zipper let him in and out and a tube that he placed in his mouth allowed him to breathe. Once the vacuum was turned on and all the air was sucked out of the bag, it would cling to him like a symbiote and nullify all sensation. Then he could sleep.

Jason took the pills from his mother, popped them into his mouth, and washed them down with the water. He then turned his back on her without saying a word and crawled slowly into the latex bag, wincing as his skin made contact with the cold metal zipper sending icy electric tingles of pain through his flesh. With another wince and a nauseous toss of the stomach, Jason recalled how he'd once fallen face first onto the floor trying to climb into the bag on his own before he got the hang of it. He laid there in mute agony for nearly an hour suppressing the urge to scream. Over the years he'd learned that his screams brought unwanted attention from his parents. His mother still had not learned not to touch or speak to him when he was in torment. Her maternal instincts would override all reason and she would run to him and try to hold him or talk to him, forgetting how much her voice and her touch serrated his nerve endings. Forgetting that the normal comforts a mother offered to her child were torture to him.

Balancing one foot on the floor while slipping the other leg into the bag, Jason eased himself into the soothing comfort of the vacuum bag. It was hooked to a wall vac and Jason had a remote control to start it up and suck out all the air once he was inside. He eased both arms into the bag while steadying his balance to keep the thing from rocking and then threw his other leg in as well. Last, he slipped his head inside and bit down on the rubber tube that would provide his only oxygen while he was mummified in the bag. He then slid the zipper shut from inside and hit the remote on the vacuum unit. The sound of the vacuum assailed his eardrums and Jason grit his teeth against the din, knowing that it would soon be over. Soon the bag was pressed tight against his skin as all the air was sucked out of it sealing him inside. Once all the air was gone the vacuum shut off on its own. Jason could not see, hear, taste, or smell anything, but the faint aroma of latex. He lay there cocooned in rubber, adjusting to the feeling of weightlessness, the absence of sensation, and the smell of the bag, until he was fast asleep.

Melanie stared at her son's locked bedroom door and felt a tug at her heart. What a cruel joke. After years of expensive fertility drugs, hormones, embarrassing exercises and sexual positions, she and her husband Edward had finally conceived a child. Then, after her son is born, she finds out that the child she'd carried for nine-months, the one she dreamed of having since she was a little girl, the one that was supposed to give her the love her own parents and even her husband had been unable to give her, that eternal unconditional love a boy has for his mother, abhors her touch. Her love could only bring him misery.

Tears dripped from Melanie's eyes as she recalled how hard she'd tried to deny the truth. Even after the doctors told her about Jason's condition she'd still tried to hold him and sing to him.

What child doesn't like to be rocked in his mother's arms? What child doesn't like to be sang to sleep while snuggled against his mother's breast? Why can't I have a normal son!

She'd even continued trying to breast feed him. More than once she'd grown so frustrated when he'd spit her nipple out and scream that she'd slapped him. Both times he fainted and went into convulsions. When the convulsions finally ceased he would lie there barely breathing in short shallow breaths with his temperature dropping dangerously low and his heartbeat faint and slow. Melanie prayed he would survive but was afraid to take him to the hospital for fear she'd be arrested for child-abuse.

"I'm so sorry, baby. Oh, Jason, don't die. Mommy's so sorry. Don't die, please. Mommy didn't mean to hurt you. Oh, God don't let my baby die!"

When his pulse rate returned to normal she would stick him back in the little plastic bubble they had made for him and seal it up tight. Then she'd stare at him and cry, pitying herself far more than her traumatized infant.

Melanie took some steak out of the freezer to thaw. Somehow she thought that the right diet would one day cure him. She would make him a hearty steak and potatoes man like her father.

Growing impatient, she ran hot water over the steak to speed up the thawing process then peeled it off of the little Styrofoam tray it was frozen to and tossed the whole thing into a pot of boiling water along with some potatoes. She cast another glance at her son's hermetically sealed door and let out a sigh as that familiar distress and longing lanced through her heart before returning to prepare her meal. She took two more pieces of steak out of the refrigerator. These however, were seasoned with cracked pepper and onions and placed in the oven for her and her husband.

At first Melanie and her husband had tried to eat like their son out of sympathy for him or perhaps even as self-punishment. More than once Edward had commented that he didn't think it was fair that they should be happy while their son suffered. They had even stopped having sex. Edward didn't want to risk having another defective offspring, and felt guilty over the pleasure she brought him. Their son would never know such joy. After a few years they went back to their old habits. They began seasoning their food again, though not as flavorfully as before. The overwhelming smell of the spices made Jason's stomach uneasy and sometimes caused him to regurgitate. They didn't fry their food anymore either, but at least they no longer boiled everything and occasionally they even ordered take-out. They were already sacrificing enough for their son. No need to make even their meals a misery.

Their sex life returned in a way. Only now it was accompanied by latex and estrogen pills. Sometimes her husband cried during sex. Sometimes she did as well. They couldn't help but to remember when the act was filled with love and anticipation. When they would imagine that each seed had the possibility of conceiving a bundle of joy to complete their family. Now their bundle of joy lay in the room across the hall mummified in latex in fear that someone or something might touch him and make him scream.

Melanie turned on the T.V. She flipped to one of her favorite talk shows and watched as the well-built and clean-shaven black host leaned in close as if captivated by the words of his guest, a diminutive Asian man in an orange robe. Melanie had always had a thing for black men. At one time she'd dated them almost exclusively. That was just one of the many secrets she'd never shared with Edward. He had enough burdens to carry than to worry about how he stacked up next to the black stallions that had mounted her in the past, especially now that their sex-life had been reduced to a cold sterile bodily function like urinating or taking a shit. Merely a necessity to relieve the pressure of the sex-drive rather than something done from genuine passion or desire.

Melanie turned up the sound.

"...Yes, this is true. The pain was excruciating, but I was able to block it out through meditation, creative visualization,

and proper breathing techniques. I survived being trapped beneath an avalanche for six days with two broken legs and a broken arm. The mud-slide knocked me right off my bike and smashed me into every rock and boulder on the mountain. I also had broken ribs, three broken fingers, and a deep laceration across my forehead. I was dizzy, in terrific pain, and freezing to death beneath the mud. I finally dug my way out using my one good arm, set the bones in my legs and arm myself and splinted them with tree branches and shoe laces, then crawled back up the mountain to the road. I tried to keep my mind focused outside myself. I imagined that I was the birds overhead or the rodents and insects burrowing through the soil. But I couldn't just envision it like a child playing make-believe. I had to believe it in my soul. I had to try to transport myself into their bodies and outside my own. It's what they teach you to do at the temple but it wasn't working. I couldn't escape my own broken flesh. So, instead of fleeing from myself I went deeper into myself. I dove into the pain, accepted and embraced it. I took away its power by welcoming it and making peace with it. Soon it held no more fear for me than the splash of a raindrop or the chill of the morning breeze. I had conquered it completely.

"One of the bones in my leg was badly shattered and had poked through the muscle. It had severed several large veins and ruptured the surface of the skin. I was suffering from hypothermia from the frigid mud and rain. My leg and forehead wounds were bleeding badly. I was losing blood rapidly and going into shock. Yet by welcoming the pain, by not fighting or resisting it and allowing myself to feel levels of anguish that our minds usually shield us from, overwhelming my senses with it until they could feel nothing more, the way a word constantly repeated loses all meaning, I was able to slow my breathing and heart-rate. That's the only way I survived. If I hadn't been able to alter my thinking I would have been defeated. Now I've perfected and enhanced these techniques. I'm using them to help cancer patients cope with the strain and discomfort of chemotherapy. I also teach these techniques to burn patients who can't be helped by morphine

or other pain medications. There have been people who have undergone surgery using nothing but my visualization techniques and no other anesthesia."

Melanie listened in awe. She felt her first genuine swell of hope in years. Could this man possibly help her little boy?

As the show neared conclusion, she rushed to gather a pen and paper to write down the man's contact information. All they listed was an email address, a website, and a name. Yogi Arjunda at www.physicalenlightenment.com.

"Physical enlightenment?"

She'd heard of spiritual enlightenment but she had no idea how someone could be physically enlightened. Still, if there was a possibility that Yogi Arjunda and his meditation techniques might allow her to one day embrace her son, she had to give it a try. She jotted the email address down and raced to the computer.

Dear Yogi Arjunda,

You are a gift from God. I hope that you might have the answer to my prayers. I listened to you describe how you overcame broken bones and frigid temperatures through meditation techniques and how you are teaching others to combat pain using similar methods and I knew I had to contact you. I am the mother of a teenaged boy who has suffered indescribable pain his entire life. He is afflicted with a rare neurological disorder that makes everything he touches, tastes, hears, sees, or smells painful to him. He spends everyday locked inside a soundproof room, sealed in a latex sensory deprivation bag, doped up on a cocktail of pain-killing medications. He has never been able to go outside and play like other children or even watch television or listen to music. Even the sound of a human's voice hurts him. I can't even touch him. I dream of one day being able to hold my son in my arms. I believe that you can help me and my family. Please contact me. I am desperate.

Sincerely,
Melanie Thompson
P.S. We will pay any price for your assistance.

Melanie pressed send and the shut off the computer. She didn't know why she added that last bit. She and her husband were comfortable, but far from wealthy. If the Yogi asked for a million dollars there would be no way she could come up with it, even if they sold their house. She was hoping that since he was a spiritual man that he would do it out of the kindness of his heart or for some nominal fee. Maybe he'd make her join his religion. She didn't care what his price was as long as he could help her and her child.

By the time she'd finished dinner, Edward was walking through the front door. She'd wanted to keep the news about Yogi Arjunda to herself until he had at least replied to her email, but seeing the dejected look on Edward's face made her want to share the good news. He looked like he was desperately in need of some.

"Guess what, Edward. Something wonderful happened today!" She was beaming when she spoke.

Edward lifted one eyelid quizzically and then turned to look at his son's door as if he expected the boy to come bursting out and run into his arms. His face then fell back into that morose grimace that had taken up residence on it seventeen years ago and refused to vacate.

"I saw a man on a talk show today that helps people deal with pain through meditation. He's helped hundreds of people, mostly burn patients and cancer patients. He said that people have even undergone surgery without anesthesia just using his techniques. I wrote to him today. I think he might be able to help Jason."

"That-that's great, honey," Edward stammered, but his face remained unchanged. He walked over to the couch and collapsed down into it.

Melanie hadn't really noticed how much the years had changed him. Once, Edward had been an enormous man. Not fat but burly, tall, broad-shouldered, and barrel-chested. Now he was a thin wisp of a man. His shoulders were bowed and stooped, curled inward towards each other. His thick chest had sunken in and his weight had dropped dramatically. His head hung low and his eyes were dull and hollow as if his body had somehow learned the trick of remaining animate without a life-force. Merely the shambling ghost of the man she had married.

"Edward, this might work. Don't just dismiss it. We have to have hope. The least you can do is give it a chance."

"And if he can't help us?"

"Then we try something else and we keep trying until we find a cure for our boy!"

"And if there is no cure? If no one can help him?"

"Don't say it, Edward. Don't you even think it! *That* is not an option." She glared at him threateningly until he dropped his head and looked away, which didn't take long. His spirit had been broken long ago on the day their son was diagnosed.

"Dinner will be ready soon. You just sit there and feel sorry for yourself while I try to help our son."

Melanie stormed out of the living room and back into the kitchen, leaving her dejected husband to ponder the chances of one day having a normal son and to once again debate the virtues of euthanasia.

Dinner was eaten in silence as they waited for the sun to set low enough for them to open their son's room without the light disturbing him. Melanie kept glancing over her shoulder at the computer while Edward continued looking for signs of life from his son's dark room. Neither of them tasted much of their meal. They chewed mechanically as if they were engaged in the process of waste disposal rather than enjoying a meal. They washed dishes and cleaned the table without conversation.

Edward looked into the pot where his son's meal was slowly boiling. The potatoes had turned to mush and the steak didn't look much better. Melanie had probably boiled it twice already, washed the steak in the sink, replaced the water in the pot, and boiled it again. Edward already knew what that mush would taste like when she was done. He'd tasted the flavorless gruel many times himself. Baby food was spicy in comparison.

Melanie took the pot off the fire and carried it over to

the sink. She turned the faucet all the way to cold, pulled the steak and potatoes out. She ran them under the frigid water for a few minutes. They were barely lukewarm when she put both of them on the cutting board and began to chop, reducing the steak to quarter-inch bites and the potatoes to a white pulp. She then piled the tasteless sustenance directly onto a rubber placemat she had chosen specially for its texture and walked into her son's room.

Instinctively she reached out for the light switch and flicked it upwards. When nothing happened she flicked it again before she remembered for perhaps the thousandth time that there was no light in this room. It took her eyes a moment to adjust to the darkness. The black walls sucked the light seeping in from the rest of the house down into them and murdered it. When she could finally make out the outline of things, Melanie stepped inside and shut the door. She walked over to the bag hanging in the middle of the room and stared down at it. Something about it reminded her of a coffin. Maybe it was the bag's resemblance to a coroner's body bag. She'd seen them on T.V. and this looked like a more stylish version of one. Something a vampire might have in his home. With the black walls and windows keeping out the sunlight her son's room would have made the perfect lair for a vampire.

A chill went through her as her mind began to carry the idea to extremes.

What if my son is really a vampire? What if that's why he hates the light? Maybe that's why he's so sensitive, because he hasn't had any blood to make him strong.

She watched the black rubber bag rise and fall with her son's slow steady breaths and chills raced across her flesh.

Maybe that's why he's so pale? Maybe that's why he doesn't love me?

Melanie knew her thoughts were ridiculous. She was deliberately freaking herself out. But once her mind began to travel this path she couldn't force herself to detour. She began to wonder what she would do if it was true. Would she be able to kill him? Could she drive a stake through her only

17

son's heart and drag his body out into the sunlight? Or would she keep him here forever and help him find the blood he needs to rejuvenate himself? She didn't want to think about it. She shook her head to rattle the idea out of her skull like a child shaking quarters from a piggy bank.

Stop it! Stop it right now! You're just being silly, she chastised herself.

Then the bag moved.

Melanie jumped. She fumbled with the tray and almost dropped it as she backed quickly away from the bag. It took several long slow breaths to calm herself. She stared at the black bag as if expecting a monster to explode out of it. It didn't move again except for her son's monotonous breathing.

Too many fucking horror movies, she thought.

Still, her heart trip-hammered in her chest as she lowered the zipper on Jason's bag and let air in. She sat down on his latex coated bed and waited for him. Jason slid out of the vacuum bag like some type of alien larva escaping an oversized cocoon. Chills raced down her spine again watching the long shadow emerge. His feet touched the floor and he stood up in the middle of the room and stared at his mother without moving or making a sound. She half expected him to attack. Then, she remembered how sensitive and fragile he was. A harsh word would be all it would take to drive him to his knees.

He sure looks like a fucking vampire though, she thought as she stared at his pale skin and long gaunt frame.

Jason was completely naked and seeing him standing there with his penis dangling limp across his thigh made his mother blush. At seventeen years old he was not a little boy anymore.

"I brought you dinner, Jason."

His hands flew to his ears and he grimaced painfully, baring his teeth in a vicious snarl. He dropped his hands from his ears and glared murderously at his mother. Melanie had to bite down on her fist to keep herself from apologizing. She pulled her fist away and mouthed the words.

"I'm sorry."

Jason shook his head and reached for the tray, careful not to allow his skin to come in contact with his mother's. For some reason he found her touch particularly uncomfortable. Melanie turned her head as he sucked and licked the food off the tray. He hated getting food on his hands and refused to use even plastic flatware. The risk of cutting himself was too high.

Melanie wanted to tell her son about the Yogi, but she couldn't speak to him and he had never learned to read more than a few basic words. They once tried sign language but Jason had proved too impatient and irritable to learn. She sat staring at her son as he scarfed his food, wondering how the Yogi would ever get through to him.

Two days later the Yogi responded.

Melanie had just about given up hope and her mood had darkened as she ran to the computer two or three times an hour for the last forty-eight looking for some communication from Yogi Arjunda. She had just finished cooking breakfast for Jason and watching as he lapped it off his tray in the pitch blackness of his room, when she stopped by the computer on her way back to the kitchen and saw the new email come in.

Her hands shook as she dragged the cursor over to the little envelope shaped mail icon and double clicked on it. She squealed like a schoolgirl when the Yogi's email popped up on the screen.

Dear Mrs. Thompson,

I read your very heartfelt correspondence with great interest. I am so sorry to hear about the grief you and your son are going through. He has a very challenging condition and one I have admittedly not encountered before. I can only imagine what it must be like for your son to know nothing else in his life but pain and what it must be like for you being helpless to prevent it. I feel it is my divine duty to help you and your child. As long as he continues to suffer my soul will not rest as I'm sure yours cannot either. I am catching a plane to come visit you immediately. If you would allow me to stay in your home as a guest while I strive to free your child from his misery, food, shelter, and your hospitality would be the only recompense I would require.

In Peace,

Yogi Arjunda

Melanie read the email over and over to herself. It was absolutely amazing to her. They had already spent thousands on various specialists. It was hard to believe that this man was going to help them for free.

Not free, she reminded herself. *He wants food, shelter, and my 'hospitality'. I wonder why he said 'your hospitality' and not 'your family's hospitality'?*

If the Yogi wasn't a holy man she might have interpreted "Hospitality" to mean sexual favors. But, she was pretty sure that all monks were celibate though she had no clue about the Hindu faith. She really had no evidence that he even was a Hindu. She had turned on the television in the middle of the program and had never actually heard him say what faith he was. She had just assumed from the orange robe and the title.

Isn't a Yogi a Hindu priest or monk or something? She wasn't sure. Her only experience with them had been on television watching a Hindu priest squeeze himself into a 2x2 box and hold his breath under water for half an hour. Yogi Arjunda certainly dressed and acted the same way the contortionist had.

Perhaps Yogis are like Christian Priests and Pastors and there are different denominations and sects? Maybe it's just an assumed title, 'Self-proclaimed' as they say? Maybe it's an entirely different religion that just uses similar titles for its priests and monks? Melanie didn't care. If the little man wanted to fuck her in order to cure her son than she'd gladly spread her legs and welcome him inside. She'd done far worse for far less before she'd married Edward.

Maybe I'd even enjoy it? Maybe he knows some of those Tantric sex techniques I've been begging Edward to try? That Karma Sutra stuff?

20

Melanie's mind started to wander again as she imagined the olive-skinned little man mounting her. More disturbing however was the response from between her thighs. An uncomfortable moistness was starting to spread at the root of her picturing the little Monk twisting himself around her body, kissing and licking her in places Edward hadn't touched her in years. Melanie had to resist the urge to masturbate. She picked the plate up again and skipped into the kitchen.

"But what if he can't help him?" It was Edward's voice in her head.

"He'll help. I've just got a good feeling about it this time." Melanie spoke out loud to the empty room.

"That's what you said about the guy with the shark cartilage and seaweed and marijuana injections. Remember how much pain Jason went through with that guy?

"Of course I remember! But that-that was different. That guy came highly recommended by the way. He'd done amazing work with Cancer and AIDS patients. He had a PHD in neurology. How was I supposed to know he was a pot-head? This is different."

"How do you know it's different? What do you know about this guy aside from what you heard on that talk show?"

Melanie hated when Edward's voice got in her head. He was so damned rational all the time. But over the years she'd learned that he was also frequently right. She washed off Jason's tray and placed it in the dishwasher. She then walked back over to the computer.

She sat in front of the screen and stared at it for a long time before deciding what to do. She then dragged the cursor up to the search bar at the top of the screen and typed in "www.physicalenlightenment.com." In a few seconds Yogi Arjunda's face appeared surrounded by hundreds of others; men, women, young and old, from various nationalities, all dressed in the same orange robes with their heads shaved. She clicked on testimonials and read a story from a cancer patient who'd survived and even claimed to have reversed the effects of chemotherapy using meditation techniques. She read stories from people who'd been in car and motorcycle accidents, people who'd been burned in fires, people who'd gone through painful surgeries, AIDS patients, and others afflicted with diseases she'd never even heard of. All of them claimed to be pain-free thanks to the Yogi's techniques. On another page you could download streaming video of people sticking needles in themselves, in their eyelids, lips, tongues, nipples, and genitals, electrocuting themselves, and even cutting and burning themselves without pain. She'd seen this kind of stuff in books before. They were called modern primitives. It was a little extreme for her but it was impressive.

Next she clicked on the link marked "Our Philosophy" and tried to read through the complex ideology of physical enlightenment. It began talking about how everything in the universe is made of electrons and protons and how less than a thousandth of our bodies are composed of actual physical matter and the rest is just empty space. It talked about how we lose and gain electrons and protons all the time. Every time we touch something we transfer some of ourselves into it and take some of it with us. How even now we are sharing electrons with distant stars. It started getting even weirder when it began to talk about how there should be no reason we couldn't pass right through things like walls and floors. How most of our atoms do in fact pass through the objects we come in contact with and that only ions deflect the rest from doing the same. It was all above Melanie's head and she couldn't see how any of it explained how a man could hook his nipples up to a car battery or pierce his penis with a sewing needle or how it would help her son overcome a lifetime of pain. Still, she continued to read.

"We are a part of all things. Our individuality is an illusion and it is this illusion that causes us injury. Do you think the moon, the sun, or the stars feel pain? We are the universe so nothing in it should be able to harm us. Likewise nothing within ourselves should be out of our control either. Nothing in our own bodies should hurt us. We are unaware of an electron passing through us so it causes us no distress, it is our mind's awareness of pain that causes it. The illusion

our minds have created for us of separate individuals makes us think that the integrity of our bodies is being compromised when something invades it, but in reality our bodies have no integrity. They are constantly flowing and changing like the water in a stream, and our minds are the channels that determine which path that stream takes. Do you think a river winces when you skip rocks across it? Just as an electron passes through me without notice because it is a part of me a knife, a bullet, fire, and even cancer should pass through me painlessly as well because they are also a part of me."

It was a bizarre sermon but it did make a type of sense. When Melanie clicked on the link below and played the streaming video of the Yogi passing a sword through his belly and out his back without shedding any blood or showing any apparent signs of discomfort, then removing it without a scar, Melanie was convinced. This was the man to help their son. There was only one problem. How could he issue his sermon and teach his lessons to a boy who cannot even hear his words without experiencing excruciating pain?

The Yogi arrived the next day.

In person he was even smaller than he appeared on television. He was just a few inches over five feet. His skin was like sun-bleached maple with smile lines at the corners of his mouth and eyes. He looked like his skin had been leathered. His eyes were enormous in his tiny head with irises and pupils so wide they left little white around the edges. Melanie felt like she could fall down into them. She could see her own image twisted across his retinas. When she looked deeper she swore she could see other reflections as if his eyes had captured their images and refused to release them. She didn't know why she had thought he was Asian when she saw him on that talk show. He now looked Mediterranean or Indian, perhaps even Egyptian. When he smiled he revealed two even rows of perfectly white teeth. For some reason Melanie shuddered and crossed her arms over her chest. Something about his smile looked menacing, predacious.

When he spoke, it was in perfect English devoid of any accent at all.

"Mrs. Thompson?"

"Yogi Arjunda? I wasn't expecting you so soon. We haven't had time to prepare a room."

"That's perfectly all right. I will stay in your son's room. It will take me some time to reach him. I want to be as close to him as possible during this period."

Melanie wasn't sure she liked the sound of that. What if he was some sort of pervert or pedophile? She looked him over again and could find nothing threatening about him, at least, not when he wasn't smiling.

His robe appeared to be wrapped around him several times and there were sandals on his feet that looked like he'd made them by hand. His shaved head had thick veins running through it as if he were deeply troubled or thinking intensely about something. He carried only one small bag draped over his shoulder along with a flute and some type of rolled up mat made of straw.

"Uh, we don't really play any music in the house. It hurts Jason's ears."

"Then you shall know when I play this flute that he has been cured."

With that the little man walked right past her and into the house. He looked around and smiled appreciatively like a lion about to sit down for a meal of fresh killed antelope.

"You have a lovely home Mrs. Thompson. Which room is Jason's?"

"The first door on your left."

She watched the little Hindu stride purposefully towards the door and her blood-pressure spiked. She was afraid that she had made a mistake. She wanted to stop the Yogi from going into that room and hurting her baby.

"Uh…um. Maybe I should introduce you before you just walk in there. You might frighten him."

"Don't worry. I will introduce myself."

"But-but how will you communicate with him?"

"I will talk to him."

"But he can't stand the noise. Even a whisper hurts him."

The tiny monk shrugged.

"Then he will hurt. Everything hurts him anyway. It's time he learned to deal with that pain rather than run from it. Now, if you'll excuse me."

Yogi Arjunda opened the door to Jason's room and stepped inside, shutting the door behind him and cutting off any further discussion. She would just have to trust him. He knew she would be anxious wondering what was happening behind the door, but it wasn't his job to make her comfortable. This wasn't about her. It was about Jason.

"Wake up, Jason." Arjunda didn't shout nor did he whisper. His voice was firm and even.

Jason wailed as if he'd been stabbed. The black bag that enveloped him undulated. The Yogi walked over and unzipped it in one swift stroke that exposed Jason's corpse-like naked flesh. Jason stared up at the tiny Asian man in shock and horror before his expression slowly resolved itself into outrage. The Yogi slapped him across the face. His palm collided with the boy's baby-soft skin with an audible "thwack!" Jason's eyes rolled back in his head. His body curled up and began to contort as if he were in impossible agony. When he was done the Yogi raised his hand as if he would slap him again. Jason flinched and his eyes widened in fright

"Did you feel that, Jason? That was pain. What you experience when I speak to you is not. You will learn the difference. I am here to teach you."

Melanie heard her son cry out and resisted the urge to run into the room. Her hand hovered over the doorknob and her long venous fingers flexed and clenched with worry. She held her breath and listened to what would have sounded to anyone else like torture, but Melanie had grown so accustomed to her son's screams that even with her maternal instincts calling for her to intervene she was able to stop herself. She stood frozen in the hallway, her brow knitted in apprehension, fear, and deep concentration, her fingers slowly creeping toward her mouth.

25

Melanie's fingernails had already been bitten down to the cuticles and now even those went between her teeth as she listened to her son's cries. She heard him scream again and again and then finally fall silent. The insulation between the walls muffled so much of the noise within that even with her ear pressed right up against the door it was hard for her to hear much of what was going on inside. After Jason's wails and cries subsided to a series of low moans she could hear the Yogi's voice steady and persistent. His voice was low but far from a whisper. Still, Jason did not scream again even though she knew the sound must be deafening to him.

As Melanie strained to hear through the solid-core door, a sound came from within her son's room that chilled her worse than his screams ever had. She heard her son laugh. She didn't know how she could be so certain that it was Jason and not the Yogi since he'd never made the sound before, but somehow she knew. This time she did grab hold of the doorknob. She started to turn it and felt the latch disengage from the strike-plate and the door creep open. She let out a cry as the doorknob turned in her hand and the door jerked out of her grasp and slammed shut. Melanie stood trembling in the hallway, staring at the closed door as the laughter continued. It had been a long time since Melanie had heard anyone in the house laugh, but she could remember the sound. And she was sure that it wasn't supposed to sound that way. The cackling that echoed from within the room was even more tortured than the screams had been. It was the sound of a mind breaking apart, ego shattering against id, the voice of insanity.

"Stop it, Jason. I don't want to hurt you further, at the moment, but I can and I will. Get a hold of yourself and trust that I am here to help you."

The little monk placed a hand on Jason's face to calm him and Jason instinctively flinched away. Arjunda smacked him again. Jason fell to the floor and lay there convulsing. The Yogi made no effort to help him.

"Listen to my voice, Jason, and you will survive this. I

know you think that you want to die and if that's what you want then that's what you will have because you will suffer every moment of my teachings, and if you do not learn to deal with that suffering then your body will go into shock and you will die. But you will experience terrific pain before you do. Every agony you have thought you have known in your life will be nothing like what you will experience right now if you resist me. Sure, you will die eventually, but it will be long and torturous. It is up to you."

Jason stared at the little monk and he started to laugh. He didn't know why he thought it was funny but somehow his entire life seemed like one great big cosmic joke that had now reached its punch line. Him locked in a room with this insane little man in the orange robe with his mother on the other side of the door no doubt dying to get inside to give him one of her excruciating hugs. No one had ever purposely hurt him before. Jason realized now that he had built up such hatred toward his mother while she had done nothing but try to help him and love him, inadvertently hurting him. But no one before this mad little man had ever purposely tried to injure him, and he now realized how much worse his punishment could be. His mother had spoken too loudly or touched him too often or flicked that damned light-switch but she had never struck him the way this little man did or if she had he was too young to remember it.

She had never stared at him as coldly and callously as this man did while Jason's stomach cramped and twisted in knots of pain. Even now he was sure that she would come to him if she could and cradle him in her arms, defend him against this evil man. Even though he had been so cruel to her, wallowing in his own self-pity, hating her for wanting to touch him, wanting to speak to him, wanting to love him. Jason began to cry.

"What do you want to do, Jason?"

The words exploded in Jason's head and it was like he was being bludgeoned with a baseball bat as each syllable popped against his skull. Jason had spent his entire life wanting it to end, wanting to die, but he didn't want to die this way. He never imagined that dying could be so much more painful than living. He shook his head slowly.

"I don't know what that means, Jason. You have to speak to me. Tell me what you want to do."

Jason opened his mouth and a hoarse whisper croaked out from between his parched lips.

"I-I don't want to die."

"Then you must learn how to live. We will start by getting you used to the sound of my voice. I can't teach you anything if you are constantly trying to tune me out. Here's what we are going to do. I am going to talk and you are going to listen. I don't care how painful it gets. You are going to listen. If your ears start to bleed, you listen, if your skull feels like it's going to crack open like an egg, still, you listen. I want you to feel the pain. I don't want you to resist it. I want you to dive down into it and experience as much of it as you can. I want you to think about its nature, its texture, its taste, its feel, its sound. I want you to examine why this sensation should be uncomfortable to you. Why anything you feel should cause you discomfort. Pain is your body's warning signal that something is damaging you, compromising the integrity of your body. My voice cannot injure you, Jason, so why should it be painful to you? I need you to listen and explore."

Jason listened. The pain was excruciating as Arjunda's words struck him like ballistic projectiles coming one by one without relent and ricocheting around his skull. It certainly felt like it was injuring him, but he was smart enough to know that this was not the case. Words cannot kill. He heard his mother and father talk to each other all the time and neither of them screamed out in agony the way he did. He liked to believe it was because he was a different creature than they were, but he knew this was not true either. They were the same and only he hurt like this. The Yogi was right. He had to find a way to get rid of the pain. He tried to block it out, to think of other things, but there was no safe happy place for him. Everything, his entire life, had hurt him. Everything, except for the sensory deprivation bag. He dreamt of the bag and that helped a little, but the torture continued as Arjunda spoke.

"Don't run from it, Jason. Don't try to escape my voice. That will only make it worse. You have to let yourself experience the pain. You have to listen, Jason."

It was as bad as being outside with all the sights, sounds, and smells buffeting down upon him, this man with his non-stop talking. It was not as bad as the slap had been though. Not even close. The Yogi had been right about that. That had been real punishment. This was nothing compared to that and the Yogi claimed that he could do worse.

But if that was pain then what is this? Jason wondered. Tentatively, fearfully, Jason began to take the Yogi's advice and drop his defenses. The sensations were staggering, but Jason was curious now. He wanted to know what it was that he was experiencing. What it was that had kept him miserable his entire life.

If not pain then what?

He allowed himself to experience the torturous sensations. He explored it, trying to find out what it was and why it hurt him. He was lost, drowning in agony for what seemed like hours before he suddenly realized that the Yogi had stopped talking.

"Have you found it? Have you found the pain now Jason? Do you understand it?"

"Not yet. But I am close."

The Yogi smiled at him and Jason smiled back. Then he collapsed onto his bed and lay still. The Yogi turned and walked out of the bedroom, shutting the door behind him.

"What did you do to him? Why was he screaming like that?"

"He was screaming because he was hurting. As you said, everything hurts him, my voice and his own included."

"But I heard him talking. I heard him laugh!"

"Yes. You did."

Melanie didn't know what to think. She didn't know what to do. She wanted to grab the little man and shake the information out of him. His calm aloof demeanor was maddening.

"What did you do to him?"

She looked at Jason's closed door and even though that room was always silent, after so much commotion, the silence now seemed ominous. Her eyes drifted back over to Yogi Arjunda, who stood there patiently, anticipating her questions and merely waiting for her to ask them so that he could be done with the chore of answering. For some reason it seemed to her that now she was at his mercy.

"Can-can I see him?"

It was the question he'd obviously been waiting for.

"No. It's too soon."

Melanie's mind reeled.

"What do you mean I can't see my own son? You can't be serious!"

"If you do not calm down I will leave right now, and after what your son has just gone through he needs me. If I were to leave at this point, he would be much worse off than when I arrived. If you want to help your son, then you will stay away from him until I say otherwise. If you do not want my help then just say so and I will leave and you can go back to your life as it was only now with a son who knows how close he was to finding the answers he's sought all his life and who knows that you took those answers away."

Melanie stared at him with tears of frustration running down her pudgy cheeks. Her eyes darted back and forth looking for someone to help her, someone to tell her what to do. For once she wished that Edward with his annoyingly rational pessimistic voice was here, but he would not be home from work for at least another three hours.

"Don't go," she whispered.

Arjunda smiled.

Jason awoke in darkness. He was exhausted and pain surrounded him like a dense cloud muddying his thoughts. He recalled his agonizing introduction to the man who'd called himself his teacher. It was the first time in his life that there had been some sense to his pain. The first time it felt like it was achieving some purpose.

Pain is how your body warns you against danger. This is

not pain. Then what is it?

Until the little man had hurt him, Jason had never questioned his pain. He had never sought to understand it. He had been surrounded by it his entire life, but it had remained a mystery to him. He had considered the entire world his enemy and thought that everything in it was attacking him and intentionally causing him harm, including his own mother. Then the little man had slapped him and Jason had understood what it really felt like to be injured. Now he needed to find a way to free himself from his prison of misery.

The little man had told him to study the sensations and once he understood them, the pain would go away. So he tried. He analyzed and studied it as it washed over him in waves and as he dissected it he could feel it losing its power. The little man had been right. He hadn't completely conquered it, but he had learned that such a thing was possible. He could live without fear of pain. He had also learned what a terrible son he was and how much he was hurting his mother. Now, he needed to conquer his affliction not just for himself but for his mother, so that one day he could hug her and reciprocate the affection she so desperately wanted to give to him.

"This is not pain," he told himself again, but this time he spoke aloud and felt an ache pierce his eardrum. He grit his teeth against it and said it again. The pain redoubled. He said it again, louder this time, then again and again and again. Each time a sharp spear of agony lanced through his skull. Sweat and tears ran down his face as he trembled, his body tensed against the onslaught. Still, he repeated it, even louder this time. Soon he was yelling at the top of his lungs.

Edward had come home just before the yelling began. He walked through the front door and his eyes rolled backwards in exasperation when he spotted the little man in the orange robe.

"You must be the Yogi."

"Arjunda. Pleased to meet you, sir. I assume you are Edward Thompson?"

"Either that or I'm a very brazen burglar," Edward quipped sarcastically.

"Or a very brazen lover sneaking around behind Edward's back," the Yogi retorted, and Edward's eyes narrowed suspiciously. They stared at each other for a long moment before Edward spoke again.

"Okay, so what are you here for? You say you don't want any money, but I can't afford to feed you for the rest of your life either. So, if you think you can cure our son then you'd better get started."

"I already have."

"He was in there with Jason all afternoon. I heard Jason talk and-and he laughed."

"Who laughed? Him?" He pointed at the Yogi.

"No, Jason did."

"Jason? How?"

"I don't know. He won't let anyone in there to see him. There was all this screaming and I heard him talking to Jason and then Jason started laughing."

"Laughter is one way that people cope with pain."

"What do you mean he won't let us see our son?"

"I don't think it's wise right now. Jason is in a very delicate place. He needs my guidance without distractions. His is such an unusual case. I have never dealt with a child before who has never known anything but pain. I need to concentrate all my efforts on him to help him through this."

"Through what?"

"Through his pain. He has been insulated from it all his life, insulated from everything. So his coping mechanisms have lain dormant. He needs to awaken those mechanisms now and learn new ones if he is to survive. He has to throw away the crutch and learn to deal with life. Tonight will be his last night sleeping in that bag. Tomorrow he goes off the pills."

"Whoa! Whoa. You're moving a little too fast. You can't just take him off his medication. The withdrawal will kill him."

"He'll survive. And if he doesn't then at least he's out of

his misery."

Edward and Melanie both looked at him in shock.

"Get the fuck out of my—"

That's when they heard the shouts.

Jason's head felt like it was being crushed. But he knew that it was not. He knew that there should be no pain here. *"Then why was it there?"* The doctors had said he was wired wrong. But what did that mean? It meant what he was feeling was not real. It warns of no danger, it indicates no injury. It is an illusion. His life had been misery because of something that did not even exist.

"THIS IS NOT PAIN!" Jason screamed and this time the strain twisted his stomach into a knot and he doubled over and wretched up his lukewarm lunch onto the bedroom floor.

"Oh, my God!"

Edward, Melanie, and Arjunda stood in Jason's doorway staring down at him as he lay trembling on the floor in a puddle of bile and sweat. He looked up at his mother through a haze of horrific agony and smiled.

"I'm okay, Mom. There is no pain. There is no pain."

Melanie froze for a moment, startled by the sound of her son's voice. It had been months since she'd heard it. She took a step toward him then turned and ran into the bathroom to retrieve his medication. Jason screamed as they helped him off the floor. He trembled as they bathed him in warm water, cleaning the vomit off his face, neck, and chest before tucking him into bed. Melanie gave him a fist full of Darvocet and Percodan and watched as his pain slowly subsided and he fell asleep.

Jason's parents walked out of the room as if they were sleepwalking.

"I've never seen him like that before. Did you see that, Melanie? And you said he only spoke to him for a few hours?"

"I don't know what I just saw. But Jason spoke to me. Did you hear? He spoke to me." Tears coursed the fissures and wrinkles in her face down to her trembling lips.

"He was fighting it. He was fighting the pain! Didn't you see that? He was resisting it! I've never seen him do that before."

"You are wrong, Mr. Thompson. Your son was not fighting or resisting it. He was accepting it and soon he will make peace with his illness and his life will begin. Unless you still wish for me to 'get-the-fuck out?'"

Yogi Arjunda smiled again and this time it was Edward who shivered.

Jason sat cross-legged in the lotus position, doubled over with his forehead touching the floor in front of him, shivering, twitching, and trembling. It had been almost a month since the Yogi had arrived and Jason knew that they had made great progress, yet still the pain persisted. At his parent's insistence Arjunda had held off on taking their son off his medication for weeks, but now it was time. He knew that it had to be done, but still Jason missed the pleasing fog he'd lived in for so long buffering him against the indescribable suffering he was now enduring. He wanted to beg the Yogi for a pill, but he did not want to disappoint the man. He wanted to show them all that he was getting stronger. He wanted to walk out in the sun, listen to music, watch television. He wanted to run and jump, sing and dance. He wanted to love and make love. He wanted to hug his parents tight and tell them how much he appreciated them. But right now, he just wanted to die.

His stomach was a nest of eels, their razor-sharp teeth tearing at his insides, their long serpentine bodies constricting his intestines, squeezing them until his lunch came boiling up out of his throat and down through his bowels simultaneously. Once the vomiting began it exploded forth in a deluge of chunky yellow and brown, splashing the walls and floor again and again. He urinated in a steady stream and diarrhea flowed freely from his rectum. Jason didn't care. This wasn't about dignity. It was about getting through his pain.

His skin was alive with sharp stabs and pinpricks like he were being set upon by a swarm of insects biting and stinging him everywhere. His muscles contracted violently, involuntarily contorting his body as bone-wracking waves of purest agony ripped through him. In the past this would have been enough to kill him. At the very least it would have put him in a coma. But he was stronger now. He would survive.

"Feel it all. It is all illusion. Your pain, your need, your physical form, everything around you is an illusion. It is all you and you are everything. You are its master, now control it! Seize the pain. Give it definition, give it form. Make it something you can hold in your hand. Do you have it now Jason? Have you captured the pain?"

"Yes. I have it. But there's so much, it's so... huge! I can't hold onto it. It's— it's everywhere! I can't hold it!"

"You must! Hold onto it Jason. This is the greatest agony you will ever know. If you can defeat this you will be free. But I need you to capture this agony and hold onto it. Give it shape. Make it into something you can control."

"I— I have it. I have it." His voice began to calm down. His breathing relaxed and his tortured visage began to smooth out.

"Now, change it. Change it into something pleasant. Change it into something that feels good."

"I don't know what it means to feel good."

"Than you must find out. It is in you. Find your pleasure centers and stimulate them with your mind, but do not let it go. You must merge the two. You must change one into the other and make them one. Not just the absence of pain but a positive sensation, overwhelming joy. You must find that ecstasy."

"I can't find it. I can't find it. There is no pleasure. I don't know what it is!"

"Don't worry. I will help you."

The Yogi sat down and thought. He could not help the boy if he could not show him what joy was. He thought a long time before he stood up and left the room, leaving Jason alone, still convulsing in agony, his body wracked with spasms.

***

"You need what?" Edward's eyebrows knitted together in outrage and indignation. He hated to feel like he was being taken advantage of.

"Five hundred dollars."

"For what? I thought you said you wouldn't charge us?"

"It is not for me. It is for Jason. I need help to get him past this stage of his healing."

"You're not buying him street drugs are you? I won't allow it," Edward stated firmly, staring the little monk directly in his eyes while crossing his arms over his concave chest.

"The goal is to get him off of drugs Mr. Thompson. If all goes well than his treatment will be over soon. Once he has made it through the chemical withdrawal symptoms he will have mastered his illness. Then I will leave you, but first I need five hundred dollars." Yogi Arjunda held out his hand and locked eyes with Edward and then with Melanie.

"Give it to him, Edward."

"What?"

"I said give it to him. Think of all the progress he's made with our boy. I think he's earned our trust and faith. If he says he needs it to help Jason then give it to him."

Edward reached into his pocket and pulled out his checkbook. He began to scribble in it when the Yogi reached out and placed his hand over the check.

"I'm sorry, but I really must insist on cash."

Edward and Melanie looked at each other doubtfully and then turned in unison to stare at Arjunda.

"What exactly is this for?"

"It's for your son. Now, please."

"I ain't exactly got it lyin' around the house. I'll have to go to an ATM."

Edward slipped his shoes on and grabbed his car keys. He shook his head and huffed in exasperation as he walked out the door, slamming it shut behind him.

The Yogi sat down on the couch and stared at Melanie expectantly.

"What?" She looked around and then looked herself up and down, "Did you want something from me?"

Melanie remembered her initial thought when Arjunda first named his price: "Food, shelter, and her hospitality."

Arjunda continued to stare at her. His face was devoid of all expression and his enormous eyes were calm and placid like dark waters reflecting her image back at her.

"Edward should be gone for at least twenty minutes if you want me to take care of you."

"Take care of me?" Arjunda began to smile again. It was an uncomfortable thing to behold. His lips parted slowly as if a crack was opening in his skull revealing the white bone beneath, like watching a fissure in the earth split wide. Melanie shivered. She hated how he could make her feel so weak and vulnerable with such a harmless expression.

Melanie swallowed deep and steeled her nerves. Then she knelt down between the Yogi's legs and slid her hands up his thighs to his groin. She felt his organ coiled up in his lap like a snake and began to stroke it appreciatively. It was much longer and thicker than she would have expected. He could have made a killing in porno movies.

"I'll suck it for you. You can even cum in my mouth if you want."

The Yogi shook his head, looking at Melanie as if she were some misguided child doing something ridiculous but harmless. He casually swatted her hands from his lap then reached out and seized Melanie by her shoulders before she could turn away in shame.

"Hasn't your marriage to Edward cured you of this? Hasn't he shown you that you're worth more than the pleasure your mouth, ass, and vagina can bring? You're not the fat girl at school anymore. You don't have to give blowjobs under the bleachers to get the jocks to pay attention to you. No more getting passed from one guy to the next trying to prove your worth by how many men want to spill their seed inside of you. Edward loves you now. Your son loves you too. And I don't want anything from you. I'm just here to help Jason. When I am done with Jason then perhaps

I can help you deal with your pain as well."

Melanie began to cry. Tears rained down her face like a sudden summer storm, her body jerked and hitched, racked with violent sobs.

"Just fuck me! You can fuck me in the ass if you want. You can cum in my face. I'll make it good for you! Just go ahead and fuck me goddamnit!"

"No. I don't need it and neither do you."

"But, Edward doesn't want me anymore. You said that he loves me, but I repulse him. I repulse you too! I'm just an old fat whore!" Her sobs increased in intensity. She pounded her clenched fists against her forehead.

The Yogi reached out and grabbed Melanie by the wrist. He pulled her hands back down to his lap so she could feel the tremendous erection swelling there.

"You do not repulse me. I desire you, but desire is just another illusion that keeps us bound to these physical forms. I wish to transcend this body someday. I can't do that by giving in to this body's wants and desires if I am ever to overcome its needs. But, believe me it is not because I find you repulsive. I find you very attractive and so does Edward. He's just struggling right now. He can't think about his own pleasure while Jason is suffering. All he wants, and all I want, is to find a cure for Jason."

"But why? Why would you help us for free?"

"I feel that divine powers have sent me here to help him. It is the ultimate test of my theories. In him may lay the answer to all of man's woes. If I can get a boy whose every breath is agony to know joy then how difficult could it be to cure the woes of the man whose greatest affliction is the loss of a job or a love or even a loved one? These emotional pains are all trivial next to the very real torment your child experiences. Don't you understand?"

"I guess I do," she said, frowning as if forced to swallow something decidedly distasteful.

This time when the Yogi smiled it did not look quite so menacing, though it was still unnerving. It still carried that air of overconfidence and superiority. Only now she recognized it for what it was. Fake. It was the Yogi's best attempt to connect with a world that he felt no connection to. He was the enlightened one and everyone else was just an ignorant savage in need of his help. It was like watching something not entirely human trying to imitate human expression. Melanie returned the expression with equal enthusiasm. When Edward arrived she ran into his arms and hugged him so tight that they both almost toppled over.

"I love you, Edward. We're going to be all right. This family is going to be okay."

When Edward smiled down at her the expression was genuine, as real as the tears welling up in his eyes.

"Would you call me a taxi please?"

"Where are you going?"

"To acquire what is needed."

"I mean what do I tell the cab dispatcher your destination is?"

"Just tell them that I am going downtown. Shopping and sightseeing."

Edward looked at the man incredulously.

"Why does everything have to be so damned secretive? This is getting fucking ridiculous!"

"Edward! Would you just call the Yogi a cab please? It's for Jason."

Edward acquiesced as everyone in the room knew he would.

"Did you get the money?"

"No, I spent the last twenty minutes looking for an ATM just for the adventure."

"Edward!"

"I'm sorry. Here. This is just so damned frustrating. He spends all day with our son and we don't even get to know what he's doing in there. We don't even get to see our own son!"

"Thank you, Edward. Do not worry. Your son will be well very soon. Then you will have the family you dreamt of back when he was just a twinkle in your wife's eyes."

Half an hour later Arjunda was on his way to Vegas Blvd and Charleston Avenue.

As they passed the towering Stratosphere hotel Arjunda's eyes did not crane to see its apex and marvel at the thrill rides perched precariously atop it, as most every other tourist would. His eyes remained at street level.

"You know they've got a rollercoaster up there? There's a rollercoaster, a freefall ride and this new thing that looks like a seesaw that takes you right over the edge of the building. The tallest building in Vegas and some genius decides it would be fun to use it to scare the shit out of people. Can you imagine that?"

"Interesting," the Yogi replied, but his eyes still did not avert from their study of the street life.

"So, where do you want to go? Anything in particular you want to see?"

"Take me to where the whores are. Not the crack whores. I need a clean one."

The cabbie turned to look over the little man in the orange robes. He was a heavyset Greek man with bushy eyebrows and thick forearms covered in coarse black hair. He resembled Bluto from the Popeye cartoons.

"I thought you were some kind of monk or something?"

"The whore is not for me. It is for a friend."

"Still, that sounds kind of kinky."

"Can you help?"

"A good clean whore?"

The Yogi nodded in agreement.

"That will be expensive. You could get one of these worn-out whores down here for a hundred bucks, maybe less. But then your friend will be risking all kinds of diseases. You could take him to Pahrump. They have brothels up there and those girls are tested for STDs every week. Wait a minute though, there're some high-class call-girls that work out of Ceasar's Palace. They wear Chanel suits and look like regular business women. They even carry briefcases and wear their hair pulled back in ponytails with glasses on. It's all a front so that the hotel security doesn't kick them out on their asses. See, there's no hookin' allowed at Ceasar's. Everyone knows what they're up to. But what would happen if Security started throwing out every woman that walked in there in a Chanel suit? They'd wind up tossing out legitimate business women, politician's wives, actresses, and of course a boat load of hookers. It's not worth the risk so they just ignore them as long as they are discreet."

"And these girls are clean?"

"Well, all it would take is one prominent business man to complain to hotel management about catching a dick drip from some skanky tramp in their hotel to bring the entire scam to a halt. The management ignores it as long as no one complains, but how many people do you think would keep quiet with a whore running around spreading herpes and God knows what else? No, I'd say those girls are pretty clean."

"Good. How do I find them?"

"They're expensive."

The Yogi flashed the five hundred dollars.

"How do I find them?"

"Well, you can't go into Ceasar's dressed like that and asking every woman in a Chanel business suit if she'll suck a dick for a couple hundred. I've got a friend who drives limos over there. I'll give him a call and see if he can hook something up."

It took a few hours to arrange everything, but soon the Yogi was seated in the back of a limousine in front of Ceasar's Place with a whore who would have made a supermodel feel inadequate.

Arjunda had already spent half his money paying off the cabbie and the limo driver for their information so he had to call the Thompson's to let them know that he'd be needing another five hundred when he arrived. The conversation didn't go well, but they had finally agreed. It had been worth it. This prostitute was without a doubt the most beautiful woman he'd ever seen. She was Spanish or Italian or possibly Yugoslavian mixed with something Asian. Her legs

41

were long and muscular, lips full and pouty, eyes wide and intelligent. Her hair was long black and perfectly styled, nails and feet expertly manicured. Her makeup was flawless. Her breasts were clearly implants, but they were not obscenely large. They were tasteful, if such a thing could be said of silicone mammaries. She looked like a top executive on her way to close a big deal.

"So, you want me to fuck a kid?"

"I doubt it will come to that. Your slightest touch will probably cause him great pain at first, but I'm counting on you to help get him past that and give him his very first experience of genuine pleasure."

"I think I can do that."

The woman spread her legs and flashed the Yogi an unobstructed look up her skirt. She wasn't wearing underwear of course and her vagina was neatly shaved. He could smell the faint aroma of some delicate floral perfume along with her unmistakable feminine musk. The Yogi was glad that all women did not look like this. Religion would have had a hard time competing.

"I think you can too."

"Who the hell is she?"

"She is an expert in her field. Her specialty is physical pleasure, which is exactly what your son needs right now."

"Are you saying she's some kind of therapist?"

"In a sense."

"Again with all the fucking mystery! Who the hell is she?"

"My name is Sophia Arguella. You can think of me as a sexual surrogate."

Edward and Melanie looked the woman over.

"A sexual surrogate? Do you mean she's a whore? You brought my son a prostitute?"

"I brought your son what he needs. Right now he is suffering and that's all he's ever done. He can't even imagine anything else. He can't even conceive of anything physical being pleasurable and as long as that is true then nothing ever will be. So, do your moral objections override your love for your child?"

"You son of a bitch! How dare you turn this around on us like this."

"Edward, I am just stating the facts as plainly as I can. I wish I had time to be more tactful and to nurture you along through this more delicately, but frankly you are not my primary concern here. Your son is going through horrific withdrawal symptoms right now. You've heard how painful an experience that can be. Imagine how much more terrible it must be for a boy whose every sensation is pain. Maybe then you will understand why I can't waste time trying to coddle and console you. You have each other for that."

"He's right, Edward."

Edward rolled his eyes.

"As usual, right? Okay, do what you have to do."

"She does still need to be paid."

The call girl spoke up. Her voice was calm and professional, as business-like as her attire.

"This transaction sounds like it might take a while. I'll settle for five hundred for now, call it charity, but that will only buy you about half an hour. Each additional thirty minutes is going to be another five hundred dollars. Do we have a deal?"

"Damn, if that's what you call charity then maybe I should start selling my ass too!"

Edward was losing the battle with his patience.

The call girl smiled coyly.

"I know a pimp who deals in boy toys. I'm sure he could hook you right up if you're interested. You'd have to get in shape though. The market for flabby old guys is pretty slow right now. Now, do we have a deal?"

Edward's face turned from red to purple as he fought back first his embarrassment and then his rage. Melanie reached out and grabbed his arm as if she were afraid he might launch himself at the woman. The Yogi smirked and stifled a giggle. He wondered how such a sharp and witty girl could have gotten herself sucked into whoring for a living. Just another one of life's infinite mysteries.

43

"Are you sure she's clean? She's not going to give my boy some crazy disease is she?" Melanie asked fearfully.

Sophia showed Edward and Melanie a card listing about ten different diseases she'd been tested for that week including AIDS, Herpes, Gonorrhea, Syphilis, Chlamydia, and Hepatitis A, B, and C. The results were all negative and the card was signed by a physician.

"I'm tested every week. I have many regular clients and most of them are quite wealthy, some of them are even famous, and all of them are married. Sending them home to their wives with an unexplained virus would be bad for business."

"A true professional, huh? Fine, here's your money. Now go do whatever the hell you do."

Edward handed Sophia a handful of cash then turned away in disgust. Now he could no longer say that he'd never hired a prostitute before. If he knew anything at all about the life his wife led before she met him, then he wouldn't be able to say with complete honesty that he'd never slept with a prostitute either.

Melanie stood in the living room with her hands clutched beneath her succession of chins as if in prayer, watching the strange little monk walk a prostitute down the hall and into her teenaged son's bedroom. When his door opened she could hear him in there moaning in anguish. She wanted to run to him, but the Yogi cast her a look of warning before he slowly shut the door. Remembering what she'd almost done earlier that afternoon, Melanie thought it best not to aggravate the little man. Edward would be crushed if he found out about her antics. Still, she was desperate to know what was going on in that room.

"Please do not speak. He is still not used to hearing any voice but my own so hearing yours might hurt him. You may undress now also. I'd hate to see you soil that lovely suit."

When the prostitute's eyes finally adjusted to the gloom she recoiled in horror.

"Oh my God!"

Jason was a mess. He had vomited again and now blood dribbled from his nose down his face, neck, and onto his chest. The contrast of his ghostly pale skin and the spill of crimson liquid made him look even more vampiric than usual. He trembled and convulsed, curled up on the floor in a fetal position with sweat bulleting from his pores. Hearing the strange woman's voice brought a fresh volley of screams from him. His eyes flew open and locked onto hers, pleading for release.

"What the hell is wrong with him?" Sophia backed up against the wall and was trying to reach for the doorknob to escape. The Yogi grabbed her hand and jerked her off the wall.

"He's going through withdrawal. He'll be okay. Just get undressed and help me lift him up and carry him into the shower. And keep your voice down. Don't speak at all if you can help it."

"I've seen people kick from Heroine before and I've never seen anyone suffer that much! Jesus! It looks like he's dying."

"His is a special case. Now please, your assistance. Grab his other arm. He will cry out, but just ignore it. I can't lift him without help. Just be very, very gentle."

After stripping down to keep their clothing from irritating Jason's skin, they lifted him to his feet and steadied him enough to walk him into the bathroom. As soon as the water struck him Jason began to wail. The Yogi had gone to great pains to get the water as close to ninety-eight-point-six as possible, but there was no way to avoid the pain from the impact of the water itself. Arjunda picked up the soap and a washcloth and began working up a thick lather. Before he could wash Jason with it Sophia slipped the soap from his hands.

"I believe this is what you hired me for."

The Yogi nodded and backed away. Sophia soaped up her hands and began gliding them delicately over Jason's flesh. As tender as she was being, Jason still squirmed and moaned in discomfort.

"Now, Jason. Try to capture the pain again. Try to find it and hold it. Do you have it? Jason, listen to me! Do you have it?"

"Y-yes, I have it"

Sophia's hands moved down between Jason's thighs. His penis sprang to life.

"Now, I want you to take that sensation and marry it to the pleasure Sophia is about to give you. I want you to make them one, but I want you to make the pleasure dominant. I want you to let the pleasure overcome the pain."

Sophia was stroking Jason's cock now with her hands lubed up with soap. His moans began to change their octave to one she recognized well.

"Enjoy it, Jason. Feel it all."

She had one hand lightly stroking his testicles and the other gliding expertly up and down his shaft. Her lips were pressed against his chest licking and sucking on his nipples. Once the shower had washed away all the soap and grime from Jason's body, Sophia lowered her head to his swollen organ and slowly slid its entire length down her throat.

Jason's breath seized in his chest as her silken wet tongue and satiny lips sent a riot of delirious sensations through his body. Even the ecstasy she was giving him felt like torture, but not like the other pains he'd experienced. This was different. It made him feel good. It made him want more. He listened to what the Yogi had said about making all of his pain feel this way.

If this is just another sensation like all the rest then why does this one feel so different?

Jason wondered how it could feel so wonderful even while stimulating the same pain receptors the Yogi's slap had fired a month before? He concentrated on what the prostitute's remarkable mouth was doing to him. He could feel her tongue twirling along the length of his cock. He could feel it circle the head and flicker beneath the rim of it. Then he felt the orgasm begin to roil at the base of him as her mouth lowered until his entire organ slid into her throat past her tonsils and her lips were buried in his pubic hair.

It felt like he'd been struck by lightning. His body jerked and bucked. Explosions went off in his head. But it was that same delicious wonderful pain he'd felt before only magnified now, magnified to the point that it felt like it would kill him.

The prostitute looked up at him as she withdrew his organ from her mouth. She stuck out her tongue and it was coated with a thick milky cream. His penis was still pulsing and that same viscous liquid was spurting from the end of it onto her outstretched tongue. Jason watched in amazement as she licked every drop of it from his throbbing organ and then smiled appreciatively up at him. The nerve-rending jolts of pleasure intensified with each stroke of her tongue. Then it was gone.

"No. No! I want more! I want more!"

He searched the various agonies still ravaging his nervous system and could find nothing like what he'd just experienced. The withdrawal symptoms were still quite powerful, but they were nothing like the wonderful torture this woman had just put him through. He could make it the same though. The Yogi had taught him how. He could control it, reshape it, until it felt like her mouth had felt.

"You've still got another fifteen minutes. I could do it again if you want me to?"

The Yogi looked at the smile spreading across Jason's face, the first one he'd seen from the boy since that day when he slapped him, and he relented.

"Go ahead. Show him more."

Sophia stood up and took Jason by the hand. He was trembling, but his erection was as hard as it ever was and the moans coming from him were no longer of pain. She led him back into the bedroom and laid him on the bed.

"Latex sheets? Kinky. Let's play."

She kissed her way up and down his milky white skin, sucking here, licking there, and even biting occasionally. Jason thrashed, moaned, but made no effort to stop her. As she kissed him, her hand crawled back down to his cock and began to stroke him again. She grabbed a corner of the latex sheet and wet it with her saliva, then she wrapped it around his erection and masturbated him with it. Jason wailed and cried as his flesh experienced the agonies of hell and the divine rapture of paradise in one nerve-rending sensation. The next orgasm felt as if it would snap his spine and turn his mind to paste. His body arched as he ejaculated into the latex sheet and screamed until his throat was raw.

"That's it, Jason. Feel it all. Make all of your pain feel like this."

"I want more!"

Sophia laughed then rolled over on her back and spread her legs. She guided Jason inside of her and then began to work her hips. It didn't take Jason long to get the idea. Soon he was pounding in and out of her with violent force.

"It hurts! It hurts! Oh, God it hurts!" He screamed. "It feels so wonderful!"

Jason looked down at the prostitute's face as he worked inside of her and was disappointed to see that she was not feeling what he was feeling. Even with the two of them joined she could not understand his pain. He would make her understand though. He would show her the beautiful agony that she had shown him.

The Yogi watched as Jason expended himself inside the beautiful whore again and again. He was pleased with his accomplishment. He'd known that this is what the boy had needed. Now Jason would never look at pain the same way again. He'd discovered that it could be a wonderful rapturous thing. Now, he'd be able to transform all of his misery into this ecstasy.

Arjunda had to use every ounce of will within him to contain his own excitement as he watched Sophia's incredible body receive the young boy's cock. His own erection strained at the center of him and he was just about to give into the urge to reach down into his lap and satisfy himself when he heard the whore scream.

"He's biting me! Oh, my god! He's biting my face!"

The Yogi leapt up in time to see that Jason had bitten a

sizeable hole in Sophia's cheek and was now locked onto her bottom lip. Sophia's tiny fists pounded against Jason and this seemed to excite him further. He withdrew his cock just as it erupted spraying the whore with semen even as he ripped her bottom lip off.

The door slammed open and his parents ran into the room. Melanie froze, her hands flew to her face as her mouth stretched itself into a large "O" and her throat strained to unleash a scream. Jason, Arjunda, and the prostitute were struggling on the bed. They were naked and there was blood all over them. Edward charged over to pull his boy off the prostitute who was now missing much of her face.

"Oh my God! What did you do? What did you do?"

He grabbed the Yogi by his throat and hurled him against the wall. The prostitute screamed and Jason smiled as another orgasm tore through him and splattered the floor at his mother's feet. Melanie's own scream finally found its way free of her paralyzed vocal chords and joined the chorus of pain.

"It feels good doesn't it? The pain? It feels wonderful, doesn't it?" Jason was staring at the prostitute as she held her face and cried.

"Look what he's done to my FACE! You crazy fucker! Look what you've done to me!"

Edward let go of the Yogi and turned to look at what his son had done to Sophia. Her lips were gone all the way up to the gums along with most of her face on the left side. He could see the muscles and tendons working in her jaw as she spoke. His eyes then traveled down to his son who was covered in blood and grinning like an idiot.

"Jesus! Arjunda, what the hell did you do? Get away from my son! Get the fuck out of my house! Get out! Get out! GET OUT!"

Arjunda was rewrapping himself in his robes when Edward grabbed him by the throat once more and dragged him out of the bedroom up to the front door.

"You don't understand, Edward. It was necessary. He had to know what pleasure felt like. I don't know what went wrong, but I can fix it."

49

"You can fix it? My son just ripped a whore's face apart in my own house! What exactly are you going to fix? Can you put her face back together? Just get the fuck out!"

He opened the door and tossed the little man out onto the porch, followed by his flute and his sleeping mat. He slammed the door before The Yogi could utter another sound.

Edward took a deep breath before he walked back into his son's room. The image of that whore's face still burned in his mind and her screams filled the air. Edward tried desperately to fend off panic and figure out what to do. No matter what, he knew he had to protect his family.

"I'm calling the police! You're all going to jail and then I'm going to sue all of you motherfuckers!"

The whore was crawling on the floor picking up the pieces of her face that Jason had spit out. Melanie was on the floor in the corner cradling Jason in her arms and crying.

A deluge of thoughts and emotions crashed down upon Edward as he surveyed the carnage in his son's room. First, Edward was amazed that the whore was still able to talk through all the pain and blood and that lipless ruin of a mouth. Then he realized that she was screaming at the top of her lungs and it didn't seem to be hurting Jason at all. Finally, he saw the true miracle. Jason was hugging his mother.

Edward stared at his son in amazement as the boy looked up at him with tears in his eyes. He'd seen his boy cry many times, but these were different. It took a moment for Edward to figure out what made them so unusual. When it finally it hit him it nearly brought him to his knees. These were tears of joy. Jason was happy for the first time Edward could remember.

"I love you, Dad."

Edward knelt down on the floor with his family as his own tears began to spill down his cheeks and drip into his widening smile. He scooped both Melanie and Jason into his arms and wept as he squeezed them tight. The whore was still screaming.

"You people are crazy! You should all be locked up! That boy is a fucking monster! Look what he did to my face!"

"You can't let her call the police, Edward. We just got our son back and they'll take him away." Melanie stared deep into Edward's eyes willing him to find the strength he'd had when she'd first married him, before Jason's tragic birth had crushed him.

"Don't worry, Melanie. No one is taking Jason from us." There was steel in his voice when he spoke. It made Melanie proud. Her man was back.

He kissed his son on the head and stood up to confront the prostitute. Sophia recognized the intent in his eyes even before his hands closed around her throat. She fought for as long as her oxygen held out, which wasn't long. Soon her consciousness began to fade as pressure from Edward's hands collapsed her windpipe. Before she slipped away she thought she heard someone playing a flute. Edward heard it too. They all did. Edward could almost imagine Arjunda's smile. It was the same disturbing rictus that now scarred Jason's face. The look of something not entirely sane, not entirely human.

Killing the whore had been easy. Disposing of the body had been a true chore. Luckily, Edward had his family to help. Melanie and Jason sawed off the head and limbs in the bathtub while Edward wrapped them in plastic and carried them out to the car in a trash bag.

Surprisingly, Edward felt no guilt over what he had done. He even felt a twinge of pride as he watched his son hacking away at the woman's esophagus trying to chop through her cervical vertebrae to remove her head. Blood splattered his face and chest and covered his arms past the elbows as he worked. The look of determination in his eyes was something new. Until now Jason had always looked like a victim. Now he almost looked powerful. The only part of the whole thing that disturbed him was the erection still throbbing between his son's legs and that grin that refused to fade.

"We have to crack open her ribcage or else it will fill with gas when she decomposes and float to the top of the Lake," Melanie said as she sawed off the prostitute's last remaining limb and dropped into the tub.

"I thought we agreed to bury her?"

"Where are you going to bury her that you can be sure no one will look? Even if you took her out to the desert there are Park Rangers and Highway Patrol Officers cruising out there. All they would need is to see a pair of headlights in the middle of the desert to alert them. Then you'd be fucked."

"The same thing goes for Lake Mead, though."

"Yeah, but there are places out there where almost no one goes and it would only take you a few minutes to dump her out there."

"That's a long drive though. What if I get stopped by the cops along the way?"

"What about on your job? You do construction right? How often do they pour foundations?

"Every morning."

"They prep the pads ahead of time though, right? You could slip her in the dirt and smooth it back over and they'd just pour the foundation right on top of her in the morning."

Edward took a long look at his sweet loving wife. She was way too good at this.

Melanie locked the door behind Edward as he set out to dispose of the body. The house was quiet again. There were no more screams. But there was still blood, all over her, Jason, the bathroom. Her son's room was splattered with it from floor to ceiling.

Jason walked out of the room and stared at his mother. He was still naked and still obviously aroused. His eyes sparkled with hunger like the eyes of some feral beast. Staring at him there, covered in blood, Melanie was once again reminded of how much he looked like a vampire.

"Come here, baby."

"I'm sorry Mom. I didn't mean to get us in trouble. I wanted her to feel what I felt. It all felt so good. Painful. Terribly, terribly painful, but still good. I didn't know the pain could be so good." He smiled again and his eyes bore down on his mother like twin shotgun barrels.

"Come on, son. Let's get you cleaned up."

Goosebumps raced up Melanie's arms when she took her son's blood-soaked hand. He let out a slight gasp as her flesh made contact with his. Not the agonized moan he usually made when she touched him. This was a gasp of ecstasy. His eyes rolled back in his head and his smile widened. Something about the expression made Melanie's thighs quiver and a shameful wetness spread between them.

She led him back to the bathroom and could feel his eyes burning into the back of her skull as she led the way. She started the shower and turned back to look at him. The look on his face was unmistakable. Melanie was flattered. It had been a long time since any man had looked at her with lust in his eyes.

Melanie sat down on the edge of the tub as her son stepped in. She began to wash the blood from his arms and legs in long languid strokes, staring in fascination as it turned to streaks of pink and ran from his pallid flesh down into the drain. Jason's moans became more sensual as the soap and his mother's smooth palms caressed his flesh. He began to growl low in his throat, purring softly while she worked the lather up his thighs. A drop of semen dribbled from the end of Jason's throbbing erection as it bobbled inches from his mother's face. Melanie tried to ignore it as she began to wash his chest, but the boy's moans, grunts, and gasps were turning her on. She placed the soap in his hands and told him to finish washing himself then she sat back down on the edge of the tub trying to catch her breath.

"No. You wash it for me." Jason's eyes were on fire. He placed the soap back in her hands and guided them down to where his manhood pulsed and throbbed, gorged with blood and vibrating with want. Melanie could almost feel his desire crackling like electricity through his skin. It disturbed her and excited her at the same time.

But he's my son, She thought to herself. *My little boy.*

Except he wasn't little anymore.

Melanie thought of all the years she'd devoted to him, sacrificing her own life and career, vacations, any type of social life at all outside of this house, in order to care for him. She had loved him even when his eyes had boiled with hatred, even when she couldn't hold him, or speak to him. Now that he was finally able to reciprocate that love why shouldn't she accept all of it? Why shouldn't she have even the love he would one day give to some unappreciative young whore in the backseat of his father's car? She deserved it. She had earned it.

Melanie began to wash him. She stroked his cock with all the tender skill and craft the whore before her had. Then, just as Sophia had, she took her son's cock down her throat.

Jason screamed as the agonizing pleasure fired through his nervous system.

"Yes, mother! Yes! It hurts so much! It hurts so much! Don't stop!"

Jason came almost immediately, digging his fingers into his mother's hair and aggressively fucking her throat, moaning in inhuman anguish. Melanie moaned as well as her son ejaculated in her mouth and she sucked down his warm semen. He continued to cum while she slid his cock further into her throat, milking him of every drop of his seed. Jason's screams now were almost deafening. It was the sound of someone being murdered.

"It's so beautiful! So wonderful! It's killing me! I can't take it!"

Jason's legs buckled and he staggered out of the shower falling into his mother's arms and driving her down to the floor. Melanie held him as his body still quaked with aftershocks from the force of his orgasm. When he looked up at his mother his eyes were sparkling again with an almost religious rapture.

"It felt like I was dying. It was so powerful."

"It's okay, baby. You won't die. Did you like it? Did it feel good?"

"It was incredible. Do you want to feel it Mom? Do you want to feel what I feel?"

Perhaps it was guilt, maybe she was just caught up in the moment, but Melanie didn't hesitate.

"Yes.

***

Melanie felt her vagina tear as Jason forced his fist deeper inside of her. His tongue fluttered over her clitoris as he tore her open and little prickles of pleasure entwined with the terrible pain. His tongue whipped back and forth across her vulva, the pleasure almost as torturous as his hand punching up into her up to his forearm. Her rectum had already prolapsed under the strain of his other arm, which was submerged in her asshole up to the elbow. She could feel his two fists grinding together inside of her, separated only by the thin wall of flesh dividing anus from birth canal.

It sounded like someone plunging a toilet as Jason worked his arms deeper, thrusting violently in and out of his mother's twin orifices, ripping up into her bowels and uterus simultaneously. His fists were like battering rams rupturing veins and arteries, pulverizing her female parts. Blood, urine, and excrement poured from her in a steady torrent, splattering the bathroom floor and coating Jason's arms up to his shoulders as his mother's bowels let loose under the strain. Her vocal chords were shredded and torn from crying out. It was the first time Jason ever believed that he truly understood his mother. The first time he suspected she might truly understand him.

Melanie's clitoris was fat and swollen as Jason sucked it the way she had sucked on him. His eyes still sparkled with that feral lust. His alabaster cheeks were stained crimson with his mother's blood. Her screams became shriller as an involuntary orgasm tore through her and her kegel and sphincter muscles spasmed and tightened around her son's forearms.

The pain was terrible. But she knew that it could be worse. She knew it was still nothing like what her boy experienced.

"It hurts, baby! Oh God it hurts so bad!"

Yet, she wanted more. Even though she knew the strain would kill her, she wanted to know all the agony her boy knew. There was no way she could look at Edward now anyway, not after fucking their only son. It was better that she die like this, in the arms of the man she'd always loved more than anything else in the world, her beautiful son.

There was a brief thought of what Edward would say when he found her exsanguinated corpse bleeding out on the bathroom floor with anus and vagina distended as if she'd been gang raped by a herd of buffalo. She thought of all the friends who had kept quiet about her past when she'd first announced her engagement to this "Good Christian man" and how they would now tell him all about her years hopping from one bed to the next. They would tell him that he was better off without her and perhaps he would even believe them. But maybe he would still love her a little. Maybe just a little.

Her last thought was of what Edward would do to their son knowing what he had done to her, then there was only pain as Jason bit down on her labia and tore each tender fold of flesh free of her. And more pain as he bit through her clitoris, paused to twirl his tongue around its bulbous head one last time, then tore that away as well.

Melanie's blood spurted into her son's mouth just as his semen had erupted into her own mouth moments before. Her body bucked and jerked in a bizarre combination of ecstasy and anguish, trying to decide between orgasm and cardiac arrest, then finally combining those two as well. She smiled up into her son's beautiful dark eyes and reached out to stroke his pale blood-soaked flesh.

Maybe she had been right about him? Perhaps he was some kind of vampire or demon. Maybe all he had needed was her blood to make him whole and strong, because he no longer looked weak and helpless. With his ghostly white face drenched in blood from his mother's vagina, his smile a gore-stained horror, he looked beautiful and powerful.

"My son." Melanie whispered with a proud smile before Jason wrenched his fists out of her anus and vagina taking much of their inner-lining with him. Her heart stuttered to a halt as the shock overcame her.

"Mom? Mom? Don't go away Mom. I need you. I love you. Mom, please don't leave me. Please don't go. I didn't mean to hurt you that bad. I'm sorry. Don't go!"

Jason cradled his mother in his arms and kissed her lifeless face, weeping softly as the reality of what he had done sank in.

Sweat beaded on Edward's forehead and his eyes shifted nervously from side to side. Whenever a police car passed him he gripped the steering wheel in a white-knuckled stranglehold and stared straight ahead. If he'd been a teenaged black kid in an Escalade instead of a middle-aged white man in a Crown Victoria, he'd already be on his knees in handcuffs with a gun pointed at his temple. Even still, he knew he had to get where he was going quickly before his luck ran out.

Edward turned into the construction site, cruising slowly down an unlit street. The electricity had not been pulled to the transformers yet and so the streetlights sat dormant without power. Edward killed his headlights. He doubted that the security guard stationed two streets over would ever get out of his trailer to walk the construction site, but he figured it was better safe than sorry.

At the end of the block there were lots that already had the form boards and post-tension cables installed ready for the foundation slab to be poured. Edward pulled to a halt in front of one and removed his shovel. The moon and stars gave him just enough light to make his way onto the lot without tripping over construction debris.

He had to move a few cables in order to clear a spot big enough to dig a grave. He removed the little plastic chairs that held the cables off the dirt and stuck them in his pocket so he wouldn't have to look for them when it was time to put them back. Then he began to dig. The top eight inches was all fill so the digging went rather easily. But Edward wanted to be at least two feet deep. It took him an hour to dig through the hard packed sand and rock, another twenty minutes to fit the various body parts into the earth, and another hour to backfill it and smooth out the sand and gravel so it looked undisturbed.

As Edward worked he tried to keep his thoughts averted from the reason for his labor. He fought back the image of the prostitute's vandalized face torn and ripped into a permanent smile. The horrified look in her eyes. He tried to block out the sound of her agonized shrieks and the feel of her pulse dwindling away to nothing beneath his fingertips as he choked the life out of her. He tried not to imagine his son's idiotic grin streaked with gore and that drowsy satisfied look in his eyes. The look of a well-fed, well-fucked man reflecting on his good-fortune. All he wanted to think about was how happy his family would be now that Jason was better.

He still could not believe the Yogi had done it. He wished he had been able to thank the little man, but instead he'd had to throw him out. What else could he have done? The man had brought a whore into his home and turned his son into—into what? He wasn't sure. He was afraid to speculate. He just wanted to get home to his family without getting arrested. Then he would sit and think and figure out how to fix everything. Everything would work out fine. He was sure of it.

Edward finished grading the pad and replacing the PT cables, setting them neatly back on the little plastic chairs, then he stalked back over to his car, sweating and exhausted, and began the long drive home.

There was still blood everywhere when Edward walked through the front door. The carpet was streaked with it all the way up to the front door. He'd assumed that Melanie would have taken care of that while he was out burying the whore's corpse. But he stifled his annoyance remembering that his wife had just received her first hug from her son in seventeen years.

She's probably still in there cradling him in her arms. She's probably even whispering him a bedtime story like she'd wanted to do since he was an infant, Edward thought.

Edward shut the door behind him and walked through the living room into the hallway. The smell of blood was enormous, accompanied by the slaughterhouse stench of meat, organs, urine and feces. Edward paused, recognizing the overwhelming aroma of death. He tried to tell himself

58

that it was from the prostitute they'd just disposed of, but his legs still wobbled as he shambled down the hallway overshadowed by a feeling of dread. Perhaps it was the shocking silence after all the screaming that had so recently filled the house.

"Jason? Melanie?" His voice shook and cracked. There was no reply.

Edward did not know what to think when he pushed open the door to his son's bedroom and followed the river of blood across the rubberized floor and into the bathroom. His mind refused to assimilate the information being fed to it from his senses. He could see his wife's body, clearly dead, murdered, the expression on her face one of inestimable anguish. He could see the blood and shit leaking sluggishly from her brutalized rectum, which had been torn open so far that vagina and asshole had become one ragged crater. It looked like someone had blown her open with a shotgun. His mind just refused to do anything with this information. Edward stood there staring at his mutilated wife without a single thought going through his head.

Nearly a full minute elapsed before the first thought occurred to him.

Where's Jason?

Jason knew he had done a terrible thing. Killing his mother was far worse than what he had done to the prostitute. He hadn't meant to hurt either of them. He had just wanted to share the overwhelming sensations, the pleasure he'd discovered, with them. He wanted them to understand and empathize so that he wouldn't feel so alien, so alone. But instead he had destroyed them both.

He wandered through the streets with his latex body-bag slung over his shoulder, filled with his few belongings. He wasn't sure where he was going. He still could not read, so street signs meant nothing to him. The sights and sounds of the outside world were staggering. It was hard to keep the sensations from overwhelming him. Every time a truck rumbled by he wanted to curl up on the sidewalk and scream.

When Jason first realized that he had murdered his own mother, and what his father would probably do to him because of it, his first thought had been to run. Run far away. He packed in a daze, showered again in the gore-splattered tub, then stepped out onto the front porch into the world and froze as an avalanche of sensations crashed down upon him. There he'd stood for nearly an hour, trembling in fear.

The world was so big, so loud, and there was so much he didn't understand about it. Cars whizzed down the street, lethal two-ton projectiles belching noxious fumes. Each one buffeted him with their thunderous engine noise as they passed and the force almost drove him to the floor. Their radios blared a violent cacophony that made him want to scream. But the smell was worse.

Jason felt like he was choking to death. The air in the house was heavily filtered and pure oxygen was pumped directly into his room. What they breathed out here was thick as stew. He felt like he should chew it before he swallowed it. Dogs barked, people laughed and yelled, horns blared, tires screeched, the wind blew the smell of dust and pollution, grass, trees, dog feces, fast food, car exhaust, human sweat, breath, and hygiene products. It descended on him like a dense cloud gagging him, making his eyes water and his stomach churn. For a moment Jason wanted to cry out and run back inside. Then he remembered his lessons. He'd been able to touch the woman and his mother because it had felt good then. He could make this pain feel good as well. He could convert it all into pleasure.

His mind traveled inward finding every discomfort and irritation, every ache and affliction, then collected and transformed it. The dust and pollution filling his nostrils and laying thick on his tongue became the taste of his mother's blood and vaginal fluids as she convulsed in that same miasma of rapturous agony that he'd experienced from her caresses. The riot of noise became sultry moans. The feel of the wind, the heat, the clothes on his back, the shoes on his feet, abrading his delicate skin, became loving kisses, the wet silky flicker of a tongue. This time it didn't take him long. He was getting better at it. Now the sensations were exciting even as they continued to wound him. Soon he didn't even have to think about sex at all in order to work the transformation. The pain itself became all the stimuli he needed. It now felt good on its own terms.

Jason smiled as he picked up his bag and walked off the porch onto the sidewalk with a painful erection tenting the front of his pants. He didn't know where he was going. He had no knowledge of how people got along in the world. How they acquired food and shelter. He knew his father worked to get money for those things, but he didn't know what work was or how you went about procuring a job. All he knew was that he had to get far away from the house before his father returned.

Cramps wound up through his calves as he walked. His ankles swelled. His quadriceps felt like they were on fire. Years of sitting around in his room had atrophied his muscles to the point of near uselessness. His will and his excitement over the new sensations kept him moving despite the considerable discomfort. He'd barely walked more than two miles before his legs refused to carry him further and he collapsed onto a bus stop bench and fell asleep. He was awakened just a few hours later when a girl sat down next to him.

"Hey. Can I have a seat too? What, are you running away from home or something?"

The girl looked younger than him by a year or two. She wore combat boots and was dressed all in black. Her skin was pale like his, but he could see that much of it was due to cosmetics rather than genetics or an aversion to the sun. Her nose, ears, and eyebrows were pierced with small silver hoops and she twirled a metal stud around in her mouth that was pierced through her tongue.

"I guess I am."

"Your parents some kind of freaks or something or were you the freak and they just didn't understand you?"

Jason slid over so that the girl could sit down next to him. She flopped down beside him and looked into his eyes, smiling vibrantly.

"I guess I was the freak."

"I figured. The latex body bag kind of gave it away. My name's Katie," she said, offering her hand.

Jason reached out gingerly and took her hand in his. He stroked it with his other hand then brought it up to his face and rubbed it against his cheek. He then kissed it and rubbed it against his cheek again before releasing it.

"Your skin feels wonderful."

"Wow. You are a freak, aren't you?" the girl said, looking more delighted than worried or offended. "Where are you going? Do you have someplace to stay or were you just going to sleep out here all night?"

"I–I don't know."

"Well, look. I just ran away from home a few weeks ago myself. I'm stayin' at this motel with weekly rates until I can afford a real place. It took all the money I stole from my parents just to pay for the first week though. I've been workin' at this peepshow place dancin' for dollars, but it really doesn't pay much. It's the only place I can work though until I turn eighteen. The good places won't let under-aged girls in there. The shit hole I work in never even asked. I was thinkin' about turnin' a trick to get some more money until I saw you lyin' here moanin' and groanin' and lookin' all miserable."

"Why did you leave home?"

"The old man had been fuckin' me for years and I finally got tired of it. I tried to do a Lorena Bobbit on him and cut it off, but he woke up and kicked my ass. I did manage to cut him pretty bad though, before he bashed my head into a wall and tossed me out on the street."

Jason didn't know what to say.

"C-can I touch you again?"

"You're cute, but you are damn weird. What I'm tryin' to say is that you can stay with me if you want to. The bus should be coming in a few minutes. It goes downtown and it'll let us off right in front of the motel I'm stayin' at. You're not some rapist or serial-killer are you?"

"I won't hurt you."

"Then you've got a place to stay."

"Thank you."

"You're welcome. And if you're good and don't try anything funny than maybe I *will* let you touch me again." She winked at him and stuck out her tongue. The little silver stud flashed in the moonlight.

Jason stared at it in fascination then reached out to touch her tongue. She pulled her tongue back in her mouth and winked at him again.

"Did that hurt?"

"Of course it did, stupid."

"Than why did you do it?"

"Because sometimes pain feels good you know? It helps you forget about all the other bullshit in your life. Clears your mind, you know what I'm sayin'?"

"Yes. I know. "

The bus arrived ten minutes later and half an hour after that they were pulling up in front of a dilapidated motel on Vegas blvd. Scantily clad women reeking of perfume, alcohol, sweat, semen, and venereal disease patrolled up and down in front of the motel waving at passing cars.

"What are they doing?"

"They're just trying to pay the rent. Same thing I was about to do tonight."

"How? How do they get money?"

"Are you serious? They fuck. Guys pay them to let them stick their cocks in their ass or down their throat and occasionally even in their vaginas. Sometimes the guys just want a hand-job, but most of the time they're looking for something to humiliate and abuse. These girls oblige as long as the money is right."

"And that's what you were going to do?"

"Don't get all self-righteous on me. A few days sleeping at bus stops and you might have been doing it too. You should be thanking your lucky stars that I rescued you."

Katie stormed across the parking lot reaching into her purse for her keys.

"Well, come on. Just because you pissed me off doesn't mean I'm going to leave you out here. Bring your body bag with you."

"I'm sorry if I offended you."

"Don't sweat it babe. I'm tougher than that."

The room was small and hot. The air conditioning system just seemed to be pushing the hot air around. There was one tiny twin-sized bed and two nightstands, one closet, one small bathroom with a shower, and a television set that advertised twenty-four hour hardcore porn.

Katie dropped her purse on the floor and plopped down on the bed, snatching up the television remote at the same time in one deft motion.

"You want to watch some porno? That's all this TV plays."

"I've never watched TV before."

Katie raised an eyebrow and twisted her mouth into a scowl.

"Where did you say you were from?"

"Right where you met me. A few blocks away, actually."

"And you've never watched TV before?"

"The sound of it used to... hurt me. And the light from it gave me headaches."

"Are you serious? What's your story anyway?"

Jason sat down next to her on the bed and began to tell her all about himself. About sleeping in the vacuum bag without light or sound or sensation, doped up on pain-killers. He told her about how he used to scream when his mother would try to touch him or speak to him. How he'd never been outside before today, had never heard music, or driven in a car, or watched TV.

"So you've never been with a girl either?"

"Well, not before today. My mother found this monk, a Yogi, who taught me how to control the pain. He brought me a woman today. It was his final cure. It worked."

"He cured you with sex? Wow. That's crazy. What, did he buy you a whore? How does that work?"

"I don't know. He just brought a woman to me while I

was going through withdrawal from the painkillers and she showed me how to touch and be touched without pain. Then everything the Yogi had been trying to teach me just made sense and I was able to go out on my own."

"So you ran? That's pretty deep. I've never heard anything like that before. So when I touched you back at the bus stop, did that hurt?"

"Yes and no. It felt good, but it was still painful, like your tongue piercing I guess. Everything is like that now. It all arouses me."

"So what was sex like if being touched hurts?"

"So much pain I wanted to scream forever, but it felt so good I didn't want it to stop."

"Sounds more like when I got my clit pierced. Can I touch you?"

"Go ahead."

Katie reached out and ran her hand over his face. She could feel his entire body tremble at her touch. She saw him grit his teeth against the pain and watched the sweat bead up on his forehead.

"That's trippy! What would happen if I hit you?"

"In the old days it would have almost killed me. Now, I suppose it would excite me."

Katie drew her hand back as if she was going to pimp-slap him. Jason reached out and grabbed her wrist in a surprisingly firm grip.

"I don't think I should be aroused right now."

"You're right. We just met and I should be getting some sleep. I've got to work tomorrow. Well then, goodnight. You'll have to tell me more about yourself in the morning."

"Goodnight."

Katie watched as Jason stripped off all his clothes and climbed under the covers. He was as gaunt as a scarecrow, with long, almost elegant limbs. His skin was so pale and translucent she could see his veins and capillaries through it giving it a bluish tinge. She didn't know what to make of the story he'd told her about having some weird congenital disease that made everything painful to him. But still she liked him. He looked like one of the beautiful undead bloodsuckers she liked to read about. She would have loved to fuck him. But more than that she wished he would drink her blood and make her live forever. Shrugging she undressed as well and slipped under the covers with him.

They slept spooned together with Jason's arms wrapped tight against her. At first she could hear him grinding his teeth and breathing heavily, his body tense and shivering. Then he relaxed, all but one part of him which suddenly became more prominent, poking her in the small of her back. Katie smiled, flattered. They held each other all night as they slept. They were both grateful for the other's presence despite the added body heat in the already sweltering room. At least it helped ward off the dreams.

The morning came and Jason greeted the sunrise with a scream.

"What's wrong?" What's happening?" Katie almost fell out of bed, reaching for her clothes and looking around frantically for whatever was attacking them.

"It's the sun! It burns! It's killing me!"

Katie smiled.

"Shhhh. It's okay Jason. It's just sunlight. It can't hurt you."

But his skin was already starting to blister and she could smell the aroma of cooked flesh. It made her aware of her own hunger.

"Damn. I never saw anything like that. Maybe you are a vampire? Try that trick you told me about. You know, make the pain feel good."

"Touch me. Please." Jason held out his arms to her and Katie came to him.

He kissed her face, forehead, eyelids, cheeks, nose, lips, chin, as he pressed her flesh to his. She responded, kissing his face as well before sliding her tongue between his lips into his mouth. Their tongues danced and dueled before she withdrew from him breathless.

"Does it hurt?"

"Yes," he replied in a strained hoarse whisper.

"Do you want me to stop?"

"No." They kissed again and lightening bolts of pain seared through his flesh wherever she touched him. He gasped and groaned. His body twitched and spasmed as white hot agony ravaged his nervous system.

"Are you sure it's okay? It sounds like I'm really hurting you bad."

"Don't stop." The veins popping out in his face and forehead, his eyes bulging from their sockets, his teeth biting into his lower lip, betrayed his excruciating anguish, still he held her tight to his body and kissed her shoulders and throat. Katie reached down between his legs and seized his manhood, stroking it a few times sending fresh tremors of anguish radiating through Jason's turgid flesh before slipping it inside of her.

"My God!" he exclaimed as her wet silken flesh received him. It was so powerful, so overwhelming. It felt like he was plummeting through the atmosphere after being shot into orbit and burning up on reentry.

"Oh shit! Oh shit! Oh fuck!" Katie cried out as Jason's wild shrieks and convulsions brought her closer to her own orgasm. She rocked her hips back and forth sliding his length in and out of her and grinding her clitoris against his pelvis.

She came just as he did.

"Shit! That was fucking wild! I thought I was killing you. I can't believe it turned me on so much. Your cock felt great! Are you okay?"

"I love you, Katie. I never want to hurt you."

"Don't get carried away now. It was just a fuck, an extraordinary fuck, but still just a fuck."

"You don't love me?"

"I just met you, buddy. Give it some time."

Katie started to get dressed.

"Where are you going?"

"To get us some breakfast."

"I thought you said you didn't have any money? You aren't going to sell yourself are you? Those girls get hurt.

Sometimes, they get killed."

"Damn, Jason! We just fucked once. Don't start the jealous boyfriend thing on me now."

"You're the only one I have, Katie. Everyone else is gone."

Tears welled up in his eyes and spilled down his cheeks as he remembered what he'd done to his mother. It was the first time he'd cried over pain that was not physical.

"Come on, man. I'm sorry. I'm not going to turn tricks. Now come on and let's get some breakfast. I've got enough for the buffet at one of the hotels downtown. They're only about $3.99 for all-you-can eat pancakes."

"I've never had pancakes before."

"Everything is new to you huh? Well, don't worry baby boy, Momma will protect you. Momma will teach you all about this big bad world." Katie finished strapping on her boots and stood up smiling down at Jason who was struggling to climb out of bed and into his pants. He looked up at her with fresh tears streaming down his face.

"Momma's dead, Katie. I killed her."

Katie didn't know what to think of Jason. They'd been together for weeks now and he stilled seemed so mysterious to her. She'd been teaching him to read and write and it was like teaching a child. But when it finally clicked, she'd caught him reading an entire book with a dictionary in one hand and a thesaurus in the other struggling his way through it. A few days later he was devouring novel after novel like they were candy. It was wild. Then there was the pain thing, which still turned her on immensely, his ignorance to even the most basic aspects of life like burgers and fries and alcohol and drugs, and that story about him fist-fucking his mother to death. That had really creeped her out.

She'd checked the newspapers for a few days for any mention of a dead housewife or prostitute but had found nothing. Still, she didn't think Jason was just bullshitting her. He was convinced that he'd murdered his mother and that his father had killed a hooker after Jason had torn her face off. Katie was used to guys trying to impress her with tales of murder, torture, and mayhem. Somewhere along the way vampires and serial killers had become signatures of the "Goth" lifestyle. She had to admit she did have a thing for vampires, but she'd never understood those freaks who wrote love-letters to serial killers in prison, even though Jason's story excited her as much as it terrified her. It was like the experiments they'd started doing together.

Since the moment Jason mentioned his condition and how he'd overcome it, she'd been dying to test the limits of his abilities. She'd also been curious to see if she could do it too, convert pain into pleasure. She supposed it was the same as the piercings. She enjoyed the sharp stab of pain every time she got a new piece of jewelry punctured through her flesh, especially in her nipples and clit. She was admittedly addicted to tattoos and had almost a dozen of them on her body with more to come once she had the money to spare. But the constant torture Jason seemed to suffer was unimaginable to her. So they'd begun to test it.

She must have been crazy after the story he'd told her, but she couldn't imagine him killing anyone. He seemed so fragile. Besides, he'd said he would never hurt her and she trusted him. He didn't seem capable of deceit. He was like a true innocent. So she'd swiped a scalpel from a hospital and brought it back to the motel room.

"Shallow cuts okay? Don't go too deep. We can't afford to go to the hospital."

"Are you sure?"

"You said you wouldn't hurt me, right?"

"I won't. I promise."

"Then go for it."

She was naked and Jason had the scalpel poised over her breast. His hand trembled.

"Just think about the pain. Don't try and ignore it or zone out. Try to explore it. I know it sounds corny, but you have to become one with the knife or rather accept that you are one with it, that it's a part of you. The blade, the plastic handle, my hand, my arm, my entire body, this room, everything is a part of you. So you have to accept that this sensation you are feeling is harmless. Because nothing that is a part of you can hurt you. But first you have to capture the sensation and understand it, then we can try to change it into pleasure."

"Okay. I'll try."

"It's too late to try. You have to do it or else it will hurt you."

Katie took a deep breath as Jason began to slice slowly through her nipple.

"Feel the pain, Katie. Don't hide from it. Feel it. Capture it. Define it. Give it shape and form."

"Oh my God! This is so wild!"

"Do you have it? Have you found the pain?"

"I-I think so?"

"Then shape it now. Change it into something nice. Make it feel good."

Katie was shocked when the orgasm tore through her like a thousand volts. Her body bucked violently, flopping on the bed like an overturned cockroach.

"Oh Shit! Damn! I can't believe I just came. Does that happen to you?"

"Sometimes." Jason looked away sheepishly. Katie sat up and slipped the scalpel out of his hands. Blood trickled down her chest from her bisected nipple. She whipped it away with a finger and held it up for Jason to taste it. He opened his mouth and licked the blood from her fingertip shivering as he did so. Katie loved watching the way his body trembled at her touch.

"Can I try it on you? Or would that be too much?"

"I don't know. I've never tried anything like this. You can if you want to."

"But what if it hurts too bad and it kills you?"

Jason shrugged.

"Say I attacked you and you were defending yourself."

Katie frowned.

"That's not what I meant weirdo. I don't want to lose you. I'm kind of starting to like your freaky ass."

"Do you love me?"

"Maybe." Katie leaned over and kissed him on the lips.

"Then go ahead and cut me."

Katie almost dropped the scalpel as the first scream ripped from his throat. His back arched and his muscles locked. His erection swelled, engorged to almost twice its normal length looking like it would tear through its own skin. Jason screamed again as he began to convulse. Katie cut him across his chest once more and he ejaculated into the air before collapsing onto the bed in a puddle of cold sweat.

"Are- are you okay? Jason? Jason?"

He wasn't moving, wasn't breathing. Katie put her head to his chest to listen for a heartbeat. It was silent.

"Oh, no. Oh, no. Oh, no."

She tilted his head back, pinched his nose, and breathed into his mouth.

"Please, Jason. Don't die."

Katie began pumping on his chest trying to keep blood flowing to his brain. She'd seen this happen before when her friend Xene had ODed on Special K. She'd stopped breathing and went into cardiac arrest and Katie had to perform CPR on her. It kept her alive long enough for the doctors to pronounce her dead at the hospital a day later. She hoped to have better success now.

"Come on, Baby. You can make it."

She breathed into his lungs again and this time he responded. Katie was almost moved to prayers when she saw his chest begin to rise and fall on its own. It was still a few hours before he woke up. By then Katie was a nervous wreck.

"What happened?"

"I was cutting on you— I mean, you said I could. But then you came and your heart just stopped. I thought you were dead. Don't ever fucking scare me like that again. I don't want to be stuck in this ratty ass apartment without you."

"Do you love me?" Jason croaked.

"Yeah, okay. I guess I fucking do."

Despite the toughness in her voice there were tears in her eyes when she lay down next to him. They made love that night tenderly, passionately, just like a real couple.

***

Katie had been coming back to the hotel later and later every night. She would walk in and flash Jason a tepid smile before storming into the bathroom to take a shower. After she came back into the room she wouldn't touch him right away, sometimes for hours.

"Are you okay Katie? Did I do something wrong? Do you still love me?"

Katie sneered and snorted in contempt.

"Of course I still love you. But so fucking what? We're probably both going to wind up on the streets soon. I can't afford another week's rent on the bullshit tips I get at the peepshow."

"Then what can we do?"

Jason reached out for her hand and she pulled it away and turned her back on him.

"I guess I'm going to have to start sellin' my ass."

"No. Don't do that. We'll think of something."

"Will we? Because I don't think so. I really don't think so."

They didn't make love that night. Jason lay in bed staring up at the ceiling watching the shadows grow long and crawl down the walls as the moon traveled from one side of the sky to the other. Katie moaned and whimpered in her sleep. Jason wanted to wrap his arms around her and comfort her, but she hadn't seemed to want his comfort lately. When she began to snore he climbed out of bed and pulled the rubber vacuum bag out of the closet. He crawled into it and went to sleep on the floor. That night he dreamt of his mother and father. It was the first time he had thought about either of them since he met Katie. He wondered where his father was now.

Edward left the police station and drove straight to the morgue. They were used to seeing him by now. It was the same pilgrimage he'd been making every night since he discovered Melanie's corpse and his son missing. From the morgue he'd make his way to the emergency room at Sunrise Hospital and then he'd cruise the strip.

It was difficult for Edward to believe that a boy who couldn't take a step without pain could disappear into a city like Las Vegas. There was no way the boy could have survived. Yet in almost a month there'd been no sign of him. He'd even contacted the Yogi a few times to see if Jason had reached out to him, but Arjunda had assured him he had not.

Edward parked in front of the Coroner's office and climbed out of the car. Beer bottles crashed to the ground and shattered as he opened his car door. Staggering, he walked across the parking lot and into the cold, sterile, morgue. He made his way down the hallway and walked right past the receptionist into the big freezer where all the unclaimed bodies were kept.

"Sir? Sir? Oh. It's you again. I've told you before you can't just wander back here. If your boy shows up we'll call you."

"Just let me take a look. You might not recognize him. I'm his father. I'll know him no matter what has happened to him."

"He's not here! Now leave before I have to call the cops."

Edward turned around and staggered back out the door and into the parking lot. He swooned and nearly fell as he reached out for his car door and collapsed behind the wheel. He cracked another Heineken, took a long swig, and set off for the emergency room.

He knew his son was out there somewhere, suffering. He would find him and he would do what should have been done a long time ago.

The sun had risen by the time Katie returned home from work. Jason noticed the bruises right away. The side of her face had the clear imprint of a fist on it and her neck was black and blue from where a pair of hands had been wrapped around her throat.

"What happened to you?"

"Don't worry about me. We've got the money for rent though. Just be thankful for that. I'm okay." Katie sat down on the edge of the bed and began to cry.

"Who did this to you? Who hurt you?"

"I don't fucking know his name. He was just some guy. They're all just nameless guys."

"What guys?"

"The guys I suck-off to pay the rent here. Happy now? I've been turning tricks since the day you met me to keep this place. I never intended on staying on the streets. I figured that I'd either kill myself or go back home before it came to that. But then I met you and you needed me and I started to love you and we needed the money so that we could stay together."

"But why didn't you tell me? Why didn't you tell me you were fucking other men? I wouldn't have let you do this to yourself."

"You would have rather seen us both out on the street? You can't help us. What are you going to do? Flip burgers and pass out and die the minute some grease splashes on you? I had to do it for us!"

"I could have done something."

"So what does this mean? You don't love me anymore? You think I'm some kind of whore now?"

"I don't know." Jason began to pace, rubbing his forehead trying to figure things out.

"You don't know? Fuck you, Jason! Fuck you! Get the hell out! Get out of here then!"

"No. Don't talk like that." His jaw tensed. He was feeling trapped. He couldn't think.

If she would just shut the fuck up and let me think! If she would just stop yelling! Jason covered his ears and fell down onto the bed.

"Does the sound of my voice hurt you now you fuckin' pussy? Fuck you! Just get the fuck out! You think I'm a slut. You don't want to be with me anymore, then leave!"

"No!" Jason jumped up from the bed and slashed her across the throat with the scalpel. Katie's eyes bulged as blood sprayed the front of her shirt and gushed down her throat, choking her.

"Jason. Don't." It was all she could say before he brought the scalpel down again.

***

Dear Yogi Arjunda,
   Sorry it has been so long since I've spoken to you. My world has changed so much because of what you have done for me. I have so much to share with you. I really want you to know how I feel. I apologize for what happened with the woman you brought to me and how you were forced to leave our house. I am on my own now and I desperately need to see you. I need your help.
   Sincerely,
   Jason Thompson

Arjunda arrived in Vegas two days after receiving Jason's letter.

"Please, take me to this address." He told the cabbie handing him the envelope with Jason's return address on it.

"You sure you want to go here? This ain't the nicest neighborhood, you know?"

"I'm sure."

They pulled up to the rundown motel fifteen minutes later and Arjunda saw why the cabbie had been concerned. This was not the place for a holy man. It was morning time so the prostitutes had for the most part been replaced by dope-peddlers. The few prostitutes that remained were of the very lowest quality. The opposite end of the spectrum from the one the Yogi had purchased weeks before.

"This is the place. Good luck," the driver said as he pulled into the parking lot.

The Yogi paid the cabdriver and stepped out of the car. The place smelled like alcohol and urine. Jason must have indeed come a long way to find such a place tolerable. Even with his own normal senses the air here was nauseating.

He walked over to the room where, according to the letter, Jason was staying. Arjunda knocked on the door and it creaked open on its own.

"Jason? Are you home? It's me."

"Arjunda? Come in. I want to show you something."

The shades were all drawn as The Yogi would have

expected, and Jason had gone to the further precaution of taping trash bags up to them. The only light came from the doorway the Yogi was standing in.

"Close the door please."

The air in the room was thick and humid and filled with the overwhelming stench of decay.

"Jason, are you okay? Who's that in here with you? And what's that terrible smell?"

The Yogi already feared for the worse. He closed the door and stepped over to where Jason sat on the bed cradling someone who was swaddled in blankets.

"Sit with me. I have questions to ask you."

"Who is that?"

"I have questions!" Jason shrieked. He was sweating profusely and his eyes were still bloodshot with tears.

"Okay. Okay, Jason. Ask me."

"Why didn't you tell me what it would be like? This world you and Mom were so anxious to send me out into. Why didn't you tell me?"

"I don't know what you mean. I told you that it would take a while to adjust to all the new experiences. What exactly are you referring to?"

"The pain! You, Mom, Dad, you all wanted me to conquer my illness so that I could be like normal people and love and be loved, so that I could go out into the world and experience life. You told me that what I felt wasn't normal, that there was joy and beauty in the world. You lied! All of you! Happiness is the illusion. It's the pain that's real. Joy is just a brief interval between periods of grief that just heightens and accentuates it. When I didn't know happiness I could live with this torture. If this sorrow was constant like *my* pain then maybe I could. But happiness keeps you from getting used to it. It gives you false hope so that it can crush you when all the hurt comes back. You should have left me alone, in my room. You should have killed me!"

"Jason. It's okay. This grief is the same as the physical pain. You can deal with it the same way." The Yogi had moved closer to Jason now trying to get a better look at what he had wrapped up in the blankets. The gangrenous stench increased as he drew nearer. The smell was stupefying. The Yogi's stomach was doing somersaults.

"No, you can't! I tried. Don't you think I fucking tried! This is so much worse. I'd rather be tortured than watch the people I love go away. No one ever understands me."

The Yogi noticed the blood covering Jason's arms and chest.

"Oh my God, Jason. What have you done?"

"I killed Momma and now I've killed Katie too. She was yelling at me. She didn't love me anymore. It hurt so bad. The things she was saying. They hurt so bad. I couldn't take it. I had to kill her."

Jason pulled back the blanket, revealing Katie's bloated face. The heat inside the room had accelerated the decomposition process and her body was swollen with gases. Her skin was green, purple and blue, like an infected wound. Her eyes were fixed and dilated and coated with a milky substance.

"What did you do, Jason?"

"You did it! It's your fault!"

Jason raised the scalpel as The Yogi stared at it passively.

"What are you going to do, Jason? You want to kill me for showing you happiness? Is that it? You think I've done you some injustice by not letting you rot away in that little room never feeling anything but hurt? I can't apologize for that Jason."

"But you didn't tell me about this!"

He let the blanket fall from his lap and the girl's corpse hit the floor with a thud and came apart. The body had been mutilated, hacked to pieces. The Yogi looked at the little scalpel in Jason's hand and tried to imagine how long it must have taken to undo her like that with such a small blade. Just cutting through the muscles and tendons alone would have been a chore but to slice through ligaments and cartilage to remove her limbs would have taken a great deal of time. This was more than the crime of passion Jason had described. Not just a momentary lapse in reason caused by powerful emotions. In order for him to do this Jason would have had to enjoy it. He looked up into Jason's eyes and for the first time saw the madness that had been lurking there all along. How could a boy suffer every moment of his entire life and not go insane? Arjunda saw now that it would be impossible.

"Jason—" But the Yogi could think of nothing to say. Then the front door creaked open and sunlight spilled into the room dazzling both of them.

"Back away from him, Jason."

Both Jason and Arjunda turned to look at the figure silhouetted in the doorway. It was Edward. He stood there with a rifle gripped in his hands surveying the carnage that filled the room. His expression was that same mixture of determination and defeat that seemed to have been permanently etched into his features. He looked like he had aged another ten years in the weeks since The Yogi saw him last.

"Dad?"

"I'm sorry, son. I'm sorry I didn't have the strength to do this sooner." He raised the shotgun to his shoulder and pointed it at Jason's head, then he stepped forward and placed the barrel against his son's temple.

"Thank you, Dad. I was hoping you'd find me. I love you."

"I love you too, son."

Pain ripped through Edward's belly as the scalpel cut deep into his guts. Blood and bile poured from the wound as Jason vivisected him, slicing through his intestines up to his ribcage. Jason grabbed the barrel of the shotgun and pulled it away from his head just before it went off, catching Arjunda directly in the chest and spraying his organs against the motel walls. The shotgun clattered to the floor without firing another shot.

"Why, son?"

"You watched me suffer everyday for seventeen years. Did you ever once wonder what it was like for me? You didn't kill me then because you didn't want to upset Mom. So you let me suffer. I want you to know what it felt like."

The stomach wound was fatal but it wouldn't kill him immediately. He would have hours to feel every torment Jason could imagine for him before he died. Edward looked up into his son's eyes as Jason withdrew the scalpel from his father's belly and began to carve away at his face. There was nothing rational or human in the eyes he saw staring back at him. He could never understand how the boy had withstood so much for so long. The doctors told Edward that his baby boy wouldn't live past his first year. Jason somehow lived seventeen. Each year had removed a little more of the boy's humanity, made him a little less like everyone else around him. Part of Edward's helplessness had always been that he could not understand his own child. Now he would. Now he would finally know his pain.

ABOUT THE AUTHOR

WRATH JAMES WHITE is a former World Class Heavyweight Kickboxer, a professional Kickboxing and Mixed Martial Arts trainer, distance runner, performance artist, and former street brawler, who is now known for creating some of the most disturbing works of fiction in print .

Wrath's two most recent novels are THE RESURRECTIONIST and YACCUB'S CURSE. He is also the author of SUCCULENT PREY, EVERYONE DIES FAMOUS IN A SMALL TOWN, THE BOOK OF A THOUSAND SINS, HIS PAIN and POPULATION ZERO. He is the coauthor of TERATOLOGIST cowritten with the king of extreme horror, Edward Lee, ORGY OF SOULS cowritten with Maurice Broaddus, HERO cowritten with J.F. Gonzalez, and POISONING EROS cowritten with Monica J. O'Rourke.

Wrath lives and works in Austin, Texas with his two daughters, Isis and Nala, his son Sultan and his wife Christie.

deadite press

"Brain Cheese Buffet" Edward Lee - collecting nine of Lee's most sought after tales of violence and body fluids. Featuring the Stoker nominated "Mr. Torso," the legendary gross-out piece "The Dritiphilist," the notorious "The McCrath Model SS40-C, Series S," and six more stories to test your gag reflex.

"Edward Lee's writing is fast and mean as a chain saw revved to full-tilt boogie."
   - Jack Ketchum

"Bullet Through Your Face" Edward Lee - No writer is more extreme, perverted, or gross than Edward Lee. His world is one of psychopathic redneck rapists, sex addicted demons, and semen stealing aliens. Brace yourself, the king of splatterspunk is guaranteed to shock, offend, and make you laugh until you vomit.

"Lee pulls no punches."
   - Fangoria

"Zombies and Shit" Carlton Mellick III - *Battle Royale* meets *Return of the Living Dead* in this post-apocalyptic action adventure. Twenty people wake to find themselves in a boarded-up building in the middle of the zombie wasteland. They soon realize they have been chosen as contestants on a popular reality show called Zombie Survival. Each contestant is given a backpack of supplies and a unique weapon. Their goal: be the first to make it through the zombie-plagued city to the pick-up zone alive. A campy, trashy, punk rock gore fest.

"Slaughterhouse High" Robert Devereaux - It's prom night in the Demented States of America. A place where schools are built with secret passageways, rebellious teens get zippers installed in their mouths and genitals, and once a year one couple is slaughtered and the bits of their bodies are kept as souvenirs. But something's gone terribly wrong when the secret killer starts claiming a far higher body count than usual . . .

"A major talent!" - Poppy Z. Brite

"The Book of a Thousand Sins" Wrath James White - Welcome to a world of Zombie nymphomaniacs, psychopathic deities, voodoo surgery, and murderous priests. Where mutilation sex clubs are in vogue and torture machines are sex toys. No one makes it out alive – not even God himself.
"If Wrath James White doesn't make you cringe, you must be riding in the wrong end of a hearse."
   -Jack Ketchum

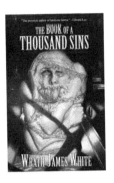

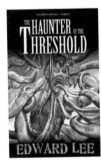

"The Haunter of the Threshold" Edward Lee - There is something very wrong with this backwater town. Suicide notes, magic gems, and haunted cabins await her. Plus the woods are filled with monsters, both human and otherworldly. And then there are the horrible tentacles . . . Soon Hazel is thrown into a battle for her life that will test her sanity and sex drive. The sequel to H.P. Lovecraft's The Haunter of the Dark is Edward Lee's most pornographic novel to date!

"Apeshit" Carlton Mellick III - Friday the 13th meets Visitor Q. Six hipster teens go to a cabin in the woods inhabited by a deformed killer. An incredibly fucked-up parody of B-horror movies with a bizarro slant
"The new gold standard in unstoppable fetus-fucking kill-freakomania . . . Genuine all-meat hardcore horror meets unadulterated Bizarro brainwarp strangeness. The results are beyond jaw-dropping, and fill me with pure, unforgivable joy." - John Skipp

"Super Fetus" Adam Pepper - Try to abort this fetus and he'll kick your ass!
"The story of a self-aware fetus whose morally bankrupt mother is desperately trying to abort him. This darkly humorous novella will surely appall and upset a sizable percentage of people who read it . . . In-your-face, allegorical social commentary."
   - BarnesandNoble.com

THE VERY BEST IN CULT HORROR

deadite
press

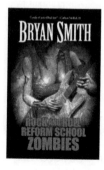

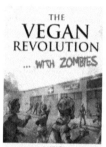

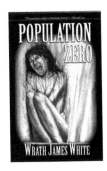

"Population Zero" Wrath James White - An intense sadistic tale of how one man will save the world through sterilization. *Population Zero* is the story of an environmental activist named Todd Hammerstein who is on a mission to save the planet. In just 50 years the population of the planet is expected to double. But not if Todd can help it. From Wrath James White, the celebrated master of sex and splatter, comes a tale of environmentalism, drugs, and genital mutilation.

"The Innswich Horror" Edward Lee - In July, 1939, antiquarian and H.P. Lovecraft aficionado, Foster Morley, takes a scenic bus tour through northern Massachusetts and finds Innswich Point. There far too many similarities between this fishing village and the fictional town of Lovecraft's masterpiece, The Shadow Over Innsmouth. Join splatter king Edward Lee for a private tour of Innswich Point - a town founded on perversion, torture, and abominations from the sea.

"Dead Bitch Army" Andre Duza - Step into a world filled with racist teenagers, masked assassins, cannibals, a telekinetic hitman, 100 warped Uncle Sams, automobiles with razor-sharp teeth, living graffiti, cartoons that walk and talk, a steroid-addicted pro-athlete, an angry black chic, a washed-up Barbara Walters clone, the threat of a war to end all wars, and a pissed-off zombie bitch out for revenge.

"Carnal Surgery" Edward Lee - Autopsy fetishes, crippled sex slaves, a serial killer who keeps the hands of his victims, government conspiracies, dead cops and doomed pornographers. From operating room morality plays to a town that serves up piss and cum mixed drinks, this is the strange and disturbing world of Edward Lee. From one of the most notorious, controversial, and extreme voices in horror fiction comes a new collection of depravity and terror. Carnal Surgery collects eleven of Lee's most sought after tales of sex and dismemberment.

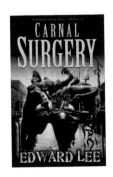

AVAILABLE FROM AMAZON.COM

deadite
press

"Urban Gothic" Brian Keene - When their car broke down in a dangerous inner-city neighborhood, Kerri and her friends thought they would find shelter inside an old, dark row home. They thought they would be safe there until help arrived. They were wrong. The residents who live down in the cellar and the tunnels beneath the city are far more dangerous than the streets outside, and they have a very special way of dealing with trespassers. Trapped in a world of darkness, populated by obscene abominations, they will have to fight back if they ever want to see the sun again.

"Jack's Magic Beans" Brian Keene - It happens in a split-second. One moment, customers are happily shopping in the Save-A-Lot grocery store. The next instant, they are transformed into bloodthirsty psychotics, interested only in slaughtering one another and committing unimaginably atrocious and frenzied acts of violent depravity. Deadite Press is proud to bring one of Brian Keene's bleakest and most violent novellas back into print once more. This edition also includes four bonus short stories.

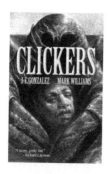

"Clickers" J. F. Gonzalez and Mark Williams- They are the Clickers, giant venomous blood-thirsty crabs from the depths of the sea. The only warning to their rampage of dismemberment and death is the terrible clicking of their claws. But these monsters aren't merely here to ravage and pillage. They are being driven onto land by fear. Something is hunting the Clickers. Something ancient and without mercy. *Clickers* is J. F. Gonzalez and Mark Williams' gore-soaked cult classic tribute to the giant monster B-movies of yesteryear.

"Clickers II" J. F. Gonzalez and Brian Keene- Thousands of Clickers swarm across the entire nation and march inland, slaughtering anyone and anything they come across. But this time the Clickers aren't blindly rushing onto land - they are being led by an intelligence older than civilization itself. A force that wants to take dry land away from the mammals. Those left alive soon realize that they must do everything and anything they can to protect humanity – no matter the cost. *This isn't war, this is extermination.*

"A Gathering of Crows" Brian Keene - Five mysterious figures are about to pay a visit to Brinkley Springs. They have existed for centuries, emerging from the shadows only to destroy. To kill. To feed. They bring terror and carnage, and leave blood and death in their wake. The only person that can prevent their rampage is ex-Amish magus Levi Stoltzfus. As the night wears on, Brinkley Springs will be quiet no longer. Screams will break the silence. But when the sun rises again, will there be anyone left alive to hear?

"Take the Long Way Home" Brian Keene - All across the world, people suddenly vanish in the blink of an eye. Gone. Steve, Charlie and Frank were just trying to get home when it happened. Trapped in the ultimate traffic jam, they watch as civilization collapses, claiming the souls of those around them. God has called his faithful home, but the invitations for Steve, Charlie and Frank got lost. Now they must set off on foot through a nightmarish post-apocalyptic landscape in search of answers. In search of God. In search of their loved ones. And in search of home.

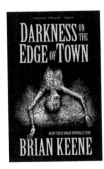

"Darkness on the Edge of Town" Brian Keene - One morning the residents of Walden, Virginia, woke up to find the rest of the world gone. Surrounding their town was a wall of inky darkness, plummeting Walden into permanent night. Nothing can get in - not light, not people, not even electricity, radio, TV, internet, food, or water. And nothing can get out. No one who dared to penetrate the mysterious barrier has ever been seen again. But for some, the darkness is not the worst of their fears.

"Tequila's Sunrise" Brian Keene - Discover the secret origins of the "drink of the gods" in this dark fantasy fable by best-selling author Brian Keene. Chalco, a young Aztec boy, feels helpless as conquering Spanish forces near his village. But when a messenger of the gods hands him a key to unlock the doors of human perception and visit unseen worlds, Chalco journeys into the mystical Labyrinth, searching for a way to defeat the invaders. He will face gods, devils, and things that are neither. But he will also learn that some doorways should never be opened and not all entrances have exits...

THE VERY BEST IN CULT HORROR

Lightning Source UK Ltd.
Milton Keynes UK
UKHW022102100120
356722UK00007B/1407/P